Dear America

MY SECRET WAR

THE WORLD WAR II DIARY OF MADELINE BECK

BY MARY POPE OSBORNE

Scholastic Inc. New York

LONG ISLAND, NEW YORK

1941

✮ ✮ ✮

SEPTEMBER 26, 1941

Dear Diary,

A cold rain is falling. The wind blows hard from the Atlantic Ocean, rattling our windowpane.

Mom and I have been living here in Mrs. Hawkins's Mansion-by-the-Sea for a week now. The name's misleading. Really, it's just a run-down old boardinghouse. Mom and I share a drafty room with heavy wooden beds, dusty oil paintings, and a ratty Chinese rug.

The other people living here are positively grim. Tonight Mom left me to have supper alone with them in the dining room while she volunteered at the Presbyterian Church, knitting sweaters for people bombed out in Britain.

Mom is good at making new friends. Unfortunately I'm not. All week the girls at my new school have shown no interest in me at all. I don't know what to do to break the ice.

SEPTEMBER 29, 1941

Dear Diary,

Good news! We got a letter from Dad today. The minute he received our new address, he wrote back. He says his ship will be leaving San Francisco any day now to safeguard the Pacific.

Mom's asleep, and I'm gazing at the framed picture of him between our beds: Dad's got a cigarette in one hand as he leans against a ship railing. His pale blue eyes seem to stare right at me, though I wasn't even born when the picture was taken.

I just wrote him a letter. I tried to sound cheerful. I kept my fingers crossed as I wrote that we're living in a wonderful place, and I have lots of new friends.

OCTOBER 8, 1941

Dear Diary,

The radio's on. Freddy Martin and his orchestra are playing "To Each His Own."

A keen thing happened today: On the way home from school, Johnny Vecchio and Bert Lyman caught up with me on their bikes. Bert is real nice. And Johnny is just about the most admired boy in the eighth grade. He has black curly hair and sparkly brown eyes. He always knows the answers in class, but never acts conceited.

They wanted to know if it was true my dad was an officer in the navy.

I told them Dad was a lieutenant commander and had been trained to be a navy dive-bomber.

"Jeepers," Johnny said. Bert said my dad sounded swell.

I told them he was on a ship safeguarding the Pacific right now, but we didn't know exactly where. I explained that we send all his mail to the U.S. Army Post Office in San Francisco; then they get it to him wherever he is in the world.

From the looks on Johnny's and Bert's faces I could tell I'd grown about a foot taller in their eyes. I expect after this conversation, things might turn around for me at school.

OCTOBER 9, 1941

Dear Diary,

I guess Bert and Johnny didn't tell anyone about my swell dad because today, as usual, the girls left me out completely.

Maxine Stone, the prettiest girl in our class, wears her hems at least two inches shorter than mine. Tonight, when Mom was heading out to her knitting circle, I begged her to help me raise my hemline. I told her I thought that the girls might be leaving me out because I don't have any style.

Mom disagreed. She said it was only because I was new and they'd all known one another for years. But she promised to pin up my skirts this weekend if I promised to stop worrying about my lack of style. "It's a deal," I said.

OCTOBER 11, 1941

Dear Diary,

This afternoon, as Mom pinned up my blue circle skirt, the lights kept blinking on and off, sending me into a tirade against Mrs. Hawkins's Mansion-by-the-Sea.

I carried on about all the strange people living here: Mrs. Hawkins, the landlady, who's nearly deaf and cooks nothing but boiled fish and watery cabbage dishes; her twenty-year-old son, Theo, a fisherman with a bad limp and a deep, gruff voice, who for some reason didn't go to school past the seventh grade; Miss Burke, a retired schoolteacher who talks all the time; and Mrs. Rosenthal and her nineteen-year-old daughter, Clara, refugees from Germany.

The Rosenthals are a bit spooky. Clara has a soft, whispery voice, and Mrs. Rosenthal seems lost in another world. She never looks directly at anybody and sometimes she talks to herself in German.

When I finished my ranting, Mom sighed impatiently. "Listen, young lady," she muttered, gripping straight pins between her lips, "I'd like you to be a little more charitable toward your fellow humans. We have no idea of the suffering others might have gone through in their lives."

She also said there's a housing shortage because so many coast guardsmen have been moved to this area. So we should thank our lucky stars we found a place to live at all.

I lifted my hands heavenward, thanking my lucky stars, and Mom laughed, all the pins falling out of her mouth.

OCTOBER 13, 1941

Dear Diary,

My shorter skirt seemed to have had no positive effect on the girls. In fact, today was my worst day at school so far. During lunch, Maxine formed a little group she named the "Star Points." She chose the five prettiest girls (including herself, of course) to be "Points."

Needless to say, I'm not one of them. I have a gap between my front teeth. I desperately need a new hairdo. And doggone it, I've got to stop biting my nails!

I suppose it should comfort me that Eleanor Roosevelt is not very attractive, either — especially around the teeth — and she's one of the finest women alive. But somehow that doesn't help. Oddly, right now I'd rather be a Star Point than Eleanor Roosevelt.

OCTOBER 14, 1941

Dear Diary,

Today Johnny Vecchio shared the front-page news with the class: The U.S. Navy is ready to arm the American merchant ships that deliver war materials to Russia and Great Britain.

This information seemed a total bore to the Star Points. But I jumped on it right away and explained to the class that German submarines have been attacking our merchant ships, so it was necessary to protect them. Protecting the ships, however, does *not* mean that we're entering into any war with the Germans — though there's still a chance we might. (Luckily, I'd heard all this on the radio last night.)

Mr. O'Malley seemed impressed. Johnny Vecchio just stared at me, his eyes shining, like he thought I was amazing.

OCTOBER 18, 1941

Dear Diary,

Mom trimmed my hair last night and put it in pin curls. Before I went to bed, I looked in the mirror and practiced smiling without showing my teeth.

This morning, I had nice, bouncy curls. I borrowed Mom's blue sweater, then set out on my bike, looking for Maxine and the Star Points. Knowing they often attend the Saturday matinee, I posted myself in front of the ten-cent store, next to the movie theater where *Citizen Kane* is playing.

They never showed up. Just as well. By the time I got back, my hair was as stringy as spaghetti.

I passed Theo and Clara sitting on the porch. Theo was saying that Adolf Hitler was a deadly microbe. Clara was silent as she shelled peas. I have no idea what she thinks of Hitler. I do know that she and her mother came here from Germany two years ago. Miss Burke told me that Clara works for Mrs. Hawkins to help pay for their room and board. I wonder what the rest of Clara's story is.

OCTOBER 19, 1941

Dear Diary,

Amazing news: This afternoon, after church, Johnny Vecchio came to see me!

As we sat on the porch steps and talked, I was so nervous, I couldn't look him in the eye. I did, however, remember to smile without showing my teeth.

Johnny himself seemed completely at ease. He asked if Dad was serving on an aircraft carrier, a battleship, a cruiser, a destroyer, or a submarine.

I told him an aircraft carrier right now, but we didn't know which one. For security reasons, the navy makes him keep that a secret.

Johnny nodded with a big grin.

He's got a great grin. It spreads slowly from ear to ear and makes his eyes shine even more. Before he left, he asked if I wanted to come over to his house tomorrow and see his war map.

Come see his war map? As Johnny says: "Jeepers."

OCTOBER 20, 1941

Dear Diary,

Johnny's war map *is* a jeepers. It's a huge colorful map of the whole world. Tiny black flags are stuck in the countries that have fallen before Hitler's army: Austria, Poland, Czechoslovakia, Denmark, Norway, Belgium, the Netherlands, and France.

Johnny and I talked about how the Nazis are now smashing through Russia.

His parents were both at work down at the cannery, but his grandmother and six-year-old brother, Bill, were home with us. After we talked about the war in Europe, I bragged a little by showing them on the map the various naval bases where we've been stationed: California, New Hampshire, Virginia, Florida, Panama, and Far Rockaway.

Every time I pointed to a different place, little Bill said, "Holy smokes!" which made Johnny and me laugh.

When Bill asked where my "hometown" was, I shrugged and said, "I guess it's everywhere."

"Gee, that's something," Johnny said.

On the way home, I realized I'd forgotten to smile

without showing my teeth. But it didn't seem to matter. I think Johnny likes me a lot — whether I have a gap between my front teeth or not.

OCTOBER 21, 1941

Dear Diary,

A terrible day today. Before the bell rang, the Star Points linked arms in the schoolyard and drifted around, singing, "I Dream of Jeanie with the Light Brown Hair." Though I was standing off to the side by myself, I made the hideous mistake of singing along with them. Maxine pointed at me, and they all giggled like I was a goon.

I can't even tell Mom about this experience. It was so humiliating. It's hard to even write about it in my diary.

OCTOBER 22, 1941

Dear Diary,

Right now I hear Clara Rosenthal singing in her room. She sings in a high, beautiful soprano, ten times better than any Star Point.

I think Theo likes her singing, too. The other night I

heard her playing the old piano in the parlor and singing for him. He stares at her quite tenderly now. Is romance in the air?

OCTOBER 25, 1941

Dear Diary,

The Rosenthals are Jewish. I learned this at an awkward scene at dinner tonight.

Miss Burke asked Clara how she and her mother were able to come to America from Germany. (Though Mrs. Rosenthal knows little English, Clara seems to know quite a bit.)

In her soft, whispery voice, Clara answered that they had come to live with an uncle on Long Island, but he had died unexpectedly of a heart attack last spring.

Did they have other friends or relatives in the states, Miss Burke wanted to know.

Clara shook her head.

Miss Burke said it was a good thing they got out of Germany when they did.

She said she'd read that the Nazis had recently given out pamphlets to thousands of Germans saying that every Jew is Germany's enemy. Any German who helps a Jew for any reason, even by showing a friendly attitude toward a Jew, commits treason against the German people. And Hitler has ordered all German Jews to wear a yellow star with the inscription *Jude*, the German word for "Jew."

"Isn't that awful?" Miss Burke said.

Clara sat there, looking ill.

Theo Hawkins glared at Miss Burke. "That's enough," he said.

Miss Burke looked surprised and hurt.

Clara said something to her mother in German. Mrs. Rosenthal started wringing her hands and rapidly asking questions, her voice rising.

"*Nein, nein,*" said Clara.

But Mrs. Rosenthal seemed very upset. Clara had to lead her out of the room.

Theo left, too, banging out the back door.

"Oh, my goodness, what happened? What did I do?" Miss Burke asked Mom.

Mom explained that she thought it was difficult for the Rosenthals to hear Miss Burke's information. "They're Jewish, you know," Mom said.

Miss Burke replied that of course she knew. She said that's why she was talking about the Jews in Germany. She thought they'd be interested in hearing about their people.

When we got up to our room, I whirled on Mom and asked why on earth she hadn't told me that Clara and her mother were Jewish. I had no idea they were Jewish. I don't think I've ever met any Jews before. If I have, I wasn't aware of it.

"It's not polite to talk about people's religion," Mom said. "It's also not polite to make Clara and her mother talk about things they don't want to talk about. So don't pry, like Miss Burke does."

I don't want to be like Miss Burke, but I am dying to know Clara's story. Did the Nazis persecute her and her family? What happened to her dad? Did he stay behind in Germany, and is that why Miss Burke's news upset them?

OCTOBER 27, 1941

Dear Diary,

Interesting news today: Maxine Stone has a crush on Johnny Vecchio. When I passed her desk, I saw she'd written something on the inside of her notebook:

M. S. + J. V.

Maxine Stone plus Johnny Vecchio?

She must be dreaming.

NOVEMBER 2, 1941

Dear Diary,

After church today, I made a point of being nice to Clara. I invited her to come up and listen to the Benny Goodman Orchestra on our radio. She surprised me by saying yes.

As we sat together in my room, I asked if she knew how to jitterbug. She didn't. I asked her if she liked Frank Sinatra. She doesn't even know who he is. Imagine!

I'm afraid I then crossed the line a little — Mom's prying line. I asked Clara if she liked living in the

United States better than in Germany. She looked at me with a strange expression. Just as I was about to apologize, she gave me a surprising answer: She said she liked Germany better — but only the Germany she had known when she was very small. She said it had once been lovely, and her family used to have many friends. But then everything changed.

"In what way?" I whispered, feeling guilty for prying.

"Every way," she said.

Just then Mom came in the room. I clammed up, feeling like an old snoop. Clara excused herself to go help Mrs. Hawkins with dinner. On her way out of my room, though, she looked back and gave me a warm smile.

Her smile made me think she didn't mind my prying too much. Maybe Clara and I can do something fun together sometime. Normally a nineteen-year-old wouldn't want to be pals with a thirteen-year-old. But maybe Clara is desperate for a girlfriend.

I know I am.

NOVEMBER 9, 1941

Dear Diary,

Before sleep, Mom and I lay in our beds and listened to the news on the radio. The announcer said that out in the Pacific, our navy was ready to move at a moment's notice. America had a striking force of battleships, their guns at the ready.

I sat straight up and nearly yelled at Mom: "What is that guy talking about? A 'striking force'? What's he mean — 'guns at the ready'? Is Dad going to *fight* in the Pacific?"

"No, no, no," Mom said. "Dad has simply gone to safeguard the Pacific. That's what he wrote us — 'safeguard.' Now go to sleep."

I tried to sleep. But it was hard. I kept tossing and turning, worrying that Dad's ship *might* end up in dangerous waters.

NOVEMBER 13, 1941

Dear Diary,

I feel better tonight. We got a letter from Dad. He said he was fine. He loves all the letters he gets from us. He reads and *re*reads them. He said he was glad I loved where we were living, and he was glad I was having so much fun at school. (Ha.) He said there was no news with him, and no news was good news.

Mom and I always feel happy after we hear from Dad. We took a walk on the beach. In the cold sunlight, we identified three falcons and two sparrow hawks migrating south. We collected some lovely shells. When fog moved in and it grew dark, we came home and made hot chocolate.

NOVEMBER 14, 1941

Dear Diary,

This morning before the bell rang, I found Johnny and Bert talking with Maxine. I interrupted them to tell Johnny we'd gotten a letter from Dad.

When he asked me what Dad had said, I couldn't help but fib a little and say, "It's sort of a secret."

Johnny immediately left Maxine's side to walk off with me. So I was forced to keep up the lie and throw out phrases like "special maneuvers" and "top secret exploratory operations." I *had* to say these things, to keep him from going back to Maxine.

NOVEMBER 20, 1941

Dear Diary,

At sunset, I saw Theo give Clara a falcon feather. She was setting the dinner table, and he came in, still wearing his waders. He handed her the feather, and in his gruff, deep voice, said, "I thought you might like this."

"Ah, it's so beautiful," breathed Clara.

Theo smiled at her — a shy smile, the sort of smile you might not think Theo had in him.

I think romance *is* in the air.

NOVEMBER 24, 1941

Dear Diary,

Mom worked at the church again tonight, so I was on my own with the others, eating Mrs. Hawkins's boiled fish and cabbage.

As usual, Miss Burke was the main one who talked. She said she thought we would soon be at war with Germany.

Theo shook his head and muttered, "No, no. It's all about to boil over in the Pacific. Keep your eye on Tojo."

"Tojo?" Miss Burke said.

"The premier of Japan," Theo said.

"I know who Tojo is," Miss Burke retorted. "But I think you're wrong about his being dangerous." She shook her head, as if she thought Theo was too uneducated to have a serious opinion on the matter.

Boil over in the Pacific?

Dad is in the Pacific.

I'd better keep *my* eye on Tojo.

NOVEMBER 27, 1941

Dear Diary,

I never thought I'd have a Thanksgiving dinner that didn't taste good. Mrs. Hawkins and Clara served us duck — duck! — instead of turkey. Lumpy sweet potatoes, kale, and of course, fish chowder. No stuffing, no cranberry sauce, no pumpkin pie.

Theo, Mrs. Hawkins, Mrs. Rosenthal, and Clara didn't mind, because they don't seem to know the difference. Mom didn't mind, because she's too nice and kind. Miss Burke didn't mind, because she was eating at her sister's in Far Rockaway.

So that just left me to mind — selfish, ungrateful, bratty me, who minded so terribly that when we all silently gave thanks before the meal, I prayed that next Thanksgiving, we'd be somewhere — anywhere — but here.

NOVEMBER 28, 1941

Dear Diary,

For days, Theo's warning — "Keep your eye on Tojo" — has been running through my mind. This afternoon I rode my bike to the newspaper stand and scanned the front page of *The New York Times* for information about Tojo. All I saw was a small article saying the Japanese have rejected conditions for negotiations with the United States.

I don't know what that means, but it doesn't sound good. I think I'd better share my concerns with Johnny.

NOVEMBER 29, 1941

Dear Diary,

I rode by Johnny's house this morning and told him what Theo had said about Tojo. He got really interested, so we took off together for the newspaper stand in town.

As we parked our bikes, I saw Maxine and the other Star Points heading into the Saturday matinee. I know they saw me with Johnny. It's wicked of me, but I enjoy being the object of Maxine's envy for a change. Give her a dose of her own medicine. Doggone it, if she were smart, she'd get interested in these war matters herself.

Anyway, on the front page of *The New York Times* was a big picture of the Japanese ambassador. It said, "Envoy in pleasant mood."

Johnny thought that was a good sign. He then read aloud a part that said President Roosevelt was taking a personal hand in the negotiations over Japanese soldiers being sent into Indochina.

I'm not sure what that means. But Johnny said it was a good sign, too, and I shouldn't worry about my dad.

Johnny's turning out to be a great friend. Could he ever be *more* than just a friend?

J. V. + M. B.?

Sometimes I wonder.

DECEMBER 1, 1941

Dear Diary,

We heard from Dad! He said our letters are the only thing that brightens his boring days. I'm glad he has boring days. I hope they stay very boring until we see him again.

DECEMBER 2, 1941

Dear Diary,

I desperately need some brown penny loafers. All the Star Points wear them. I need a wide white belt to make my waistline look slimmer, too. And I wonder if there is some kind of nail polish that tastes so disgusting, I won't bite my nails anymore.

DECEMBER 3, 1941

Dear Diary,

Mom and I walked on the empty, windblown beach this afternoon. I wanted to discuss my shoe, belt, and nail problems with her, but I didn't think it was a good time. She seemed sad.

I figure she's always missing Dad. He's been gone a whole lot during our lives, being a career navy officer. But for some reason, this time feels different from the other times. It feels ominous. Is that the right word? Ominous.

DECEMBER 5, 1941

Dear Diary,

During social studies Mr. O'Malley quoted from a newspaper column written by Eleanor Roosevelt. Mrs.

Roosevelt wants all Americans to "pledge to be a little thoughtful every day about the meaning of freedom."

Mr. O'Malley asked us each to tell the class what freedom means to us. Johnny said it meant he could read the newspaper and listen to the radio.

I said freedom meant that if I chose, I could be friends with a German Jew named Clara and no one would mind. I added that as a true friend, I would be kind and accepting and if I had a group, I would let her be part of it. I got a little carried away, I guess, trying to send a message to the Star Points.

When Maxine's turn came, she froze. She had no idea what freedom meant to her. She giggled, and like a bunch of nuts, all the Points giggled with her, changing the exercise into something silly. I thought Johnny would finally see that Maxine was an idiot. But when I looked over at him, he was laughing, too.

DECEMBER 7, 1941

Dear Diary,
The Japanese have attacked us!

Theo was right — things boiled over in the Pacific!

At about 2:30 this afternoon, Mom was writing to Dad, and I was dancing to the Benny Goodman Orchestra on the radio when the announcer broke in:

"Flash! The White House has reported a Japanese attack on Pearl Harbor. Japanese Imperial headquarters announces a state of war with the United States! Stay tuned for further developments!"

"Oh, my gosh!" Mom cried.

I threw open our door and shrieked to the household, "The Japanese have bombed Pearl Harbor!"

Miss Burke came out of her door, exclaiming, "What? What?" as she ran into our room, clumping in her big black shoes. "Where's Pearl Harbor?" she asked frantically.

"I don't know!" Mom said. "Maddie, find out where it is!"

I ran back into the hall and shouted over the banister, "Theo! Where's Pearl Harbor?"

Theo didn't seem to be home. As I started back to our room, I saw Clara and her mother standing in their doorway. They look scared, so I tried to speak calmly. "The Japanese have attacked a place called Pearl Harbor," I said. "We don't know where it is. But don't worry."

Mrs. Rosenthal shook her head nervously and went back into their room. Clara stayed in the hall.

I asked her if she wanted to listen to our radio. She said she'd better not leave her mother. I told her I'd come give her reports.

At that moment, Theo came through the front door, and I hollered the news to him.

When Theo joined Mom, Miss Burke, and me, he told us that Pearl Harbor was in Hawaii. Miss Burke didn't believe him until the radio confirmed that Pearl Harbor was on the Hawaiian island of Oahu.

Mom and I were nearly hysterical, worrying that Dad's ship might have been at Pearl Harbor. It was a relief when the announcer finally said that hundreds of ships were destroyed or damaged, but none of them were aircraft carriers. Mom grabbed me and hugged me, and we both laughed. It was terrible of us, but we were momentarily so happy — one thing we know for sure is that Dad is on an aircraft carrier.

For the rest of the day, Theo, Miss Burke, Mrs.

Hawkins, Mom, and I all listened to the radio, and I kept delivering the news to Clara:

"Early this morning, mustard-colored warplanes with red suns on their wings attacked the U.S. naval base.

"Thousands were killed.

"Invasion of the West Coast of the United States is possible.

"Men of all military services are being summoned back to duty at once.

"Now the entire world is at war."

All the time we listened to the news, I kept thinking about Dad. He's not on assignment just to "safeguard" the Pacific anymore. Now he's there to fight.

DECEMBER 8, 1941

Dear Diary,

At school today all the kids kept saying, "The Japs are coming! The Japs are coming!"

A lot of attention got focused on me because Johnny

told everyone that my dad is a navy fighter pilot who's serving in the Pacific. So far, I'm the only one in my class who has a dad in the military. But that probably won't be for long.

I explained that my dad was safe because no aircraft carriers were hit at Pearl Harbor.

Mr. O'Malley had brought in *The New York Times*, and he asked me to read it and make a report to the class after lunch. I worked on this assignment during recess (while the Star Points linked arms and strolled around the school grounds, singing "I Got It Bad and That Ain't Good" as if they didn't have a care in the world).

In my report, I told everyone that the mayor of New York City had urged the public to be on alert. He said the city was an extreme danger zone and should take every possible safeguard against sabotage. He also said the FBI had rounded up over two thousand Japanese people in New York City, and that he was putting extra guards at the tunnels, on the waterfront, and in important public buildings.

I read the Japanese Declaration of War to the class because it sounded like something from a fairy-tale book:

"We, by the grace of Heaven, Emperor of Japan and seated on the throne of a line unbroken for ages eternal, enjoin upon thee, our loyal and brave subjects. We hereby declare war on the United States of America and the British Empire."

I also read an inspirational message from Eleanor Roosevelt to America's women, and a message from her to America's young people.

You could have heard a pin drop while I gave my report to the class. I felt important, as if I myself were playing a role in history.

As soon as school was out, I hurried home on my bike and found Mom and Miss Burke in the parlor, knitting scarves for the British. I read them Mrs. Roosevelt's words to women:

"You cannot escape anxiety, you cannot escape the clutch of fear at your heart, and yet, I hope that the certainty of what we have to meet will make you rise above these fears."

For myself, I saved Mrs. Roosevelt's words to America's young people, and tonight copied them onto a piece of blue stationery and taped it to my wall:

"You are going to have a great opportunity. There will be high moments in which your strength and ability will be tested. I have faith in you."

Mom's already gone to bed. She's exhausted, I think, from worrying about a war with the Japanese and what it all might mean for Dad. I'm worried, too. I'm shivering so hard, I don't know if I'll be able to sleep tonight.

"I have faith in you," Mrs. Roosevelt said.

I want desperately to rise to her challenge. I feel like saying my prayers to Mrs. Roosevelt tonight, instead of to God.

DECEMBER 9, 1941

Dear Diary,

I copied down more information for the class today from Mr. O'Malley's *New York Times*.

During recess, while the Star Points yapped about a

Christmas dance sponsored by the women's auxiliary, I wrote out parts of the speech President Roosevelt gave to Congress on Monday:

"Yesterday, December 7, 1941 — a date which will live in infamy — the United States of America was suddenly and deliberately attacked by naval and air forces of the Empire of Japan . . . No matter how long it may take us to overcome this premeditated invasion, the American people in their righteous might will win through to absolute victory . . . I ask that the Congress declare that since the unpro- voked and dastardly attack by Japan on Sunday, December 7, 1941, a state of war has existed be- tween the United States and the Japanese Empire."

When I read the declaration to the class, Johnny stared at me like I was made of gold.

I was bushed at the end of the day and went home and crawled into bed. I feel like I'm in a fever, a war fever. What can I do? How can I help? Mom's working at the church. I wish she'd asked me to go with her. I wish we would hear from Dad soon. Please write us, Dad, as soon as you can.

DECEMBER 11, 1941

Dear Diary,

Tonight Miss Burke told us the radio had announced that Hitler and Mussolini have declared war on the United States.

"What's going on?" Mrs. Hawkins asked, cupping her hand around her ear.

"The Germans and Italians have declared war against us!" Miss Burke yelled. "War! *War!*"

Mrs. Rosenthal stood up from the table as if she were going to run out the front door.

Theo grabbed her. Then he and Clara led Mrs. Rosenthal out of the room.

I myself wasn't all that shocked to hear about Hitler's declaration of war. Ever since Pearl Harbor got bombed, the enemy has all blended together. I just pray we hear from Dad soon.

DECEMBER 12, 1941

Dear Diary,

Today, Johnny asked Mr. O'Malley if he and I could make a sign for the class. He wanted to write a quote he'd seen in an advertisement: VICTORY DOES NOT COME WITHOUT A PRICE.

A super idea, Mr. O'Malley said. So Johnny and I got to work. While we lettered the sign during recess, we discussed the evils of Hitler and Mussolini. (I borrowed Theo's description of Hitler as a "deadly microbe.") While we talked, I could feel Maxine's eyes on us. I have to confess once again, I didn't mind making her jealous.

DECEMBER 13, 1941

Dear Diary,

We heard from Dad! He told us not to worry about him. Since we are now at war with Japan, his place of duty will be even more secret than before, he said. But he's sure he won't be seeing any combat soon.

Thank goodness!

The weirdest thing was that some words in his letter were blacked out. Mom explained that the words had been censored by the military for fear they might give the enemy information if the letter fell into their hands. She said all letters from servicemen were being censored now.

At least the censors didn't black out the last words he wrote: "Please, my Sweetheart and my Doodlebug, do not worry. I am not (underlined three times) in harm's way."

DECEMBER 15, 1941

Dear Diary,

I couldn't wait to tell Johnny about our letter from Dad. I caught up with him on the way to school and told him that Dad's letter was so secret, the military had censored parts of it. I confess I didn't tell him Dad said he wouldn't be seeing any combat. I might have even made it sound a little like Dad *would* be seeing combat. But I kept my fingers crossed while I said this. Fortunately, the subject moved quickly to aircraft carriers, and I could honestly tell Johnny that I'd been on one before.

DECEMBER 16, 1941

Dear Diary,

Mom and I put together a great Christmas box for Dad and sent it to the military post office in San Francisco. Military mail is the priority mail in the country now.

We made brownies and oatmeal cookies and packed them along with some handkerchiefs and socks, and books by Damon Runyon and James M. Cain, and a sprig of mistletoe. Plus, of course, a love note from both of us, signed, your Sweetheart and your Doodlebug.

DECEMBER 17, 1941

Dear Diary,

Another letter from Dad with whole sentences censored. He told us to be brave and do all we can to help the country. We must preserve our freedom at all costs. He said, "Doodlebug, take good care of Mom and yourself. Give thanks each day that you are an American. Keep the home fires burning."

I'm aching to do something for the war effort. Aching

so bad, I feel crazy. Right now I'd do *anything* for Dad and for America.

DECEMBER 18, 1941

Dear Diary,

In the girls' room before class, all Maxine could talk about was the dress her mother is making for her to wear to the women's auxiliary Christmas dance. Apparently it's a green velvet jumper with a peppermint-pink striped blouse. For crying out loud, doesn't that girl know there's a war on? When is she going to start doing her part?

DECEMBER 19, 1941

Dear Diary,

Today I learned that life is definitely not fair.

It was our last day of school before the holidays. On our way out of the building, Maxine called to Johnny, "Hey, silly! You didn't tell me what time your dad is picking me up!"

I froze, wondering what she meant. I pretended to

fiddle with the belt on my coat, waiting to hear his answer.

"What time is that dance?" he said.

Then I understood completely. It was as clear as a bell. My face got so red, I felt as if I were about to explode. I could hardly find my bike in the bike rack. When I did, I jumped on it and pedaled fast for home, trying to get there before the dam broke.

So Johnny's taking Maxine to the Christmas dance sponsored by the women's auxiliary. I've been a dope. All this time I was sure he preferred me over Maxine. I thought I had so much more to offer than her — brains, war knowledge, a military dad. But now I realize winning someone like Johnny is about being beautiful and having a slim waistline and penny loafers. It doesn't matter if you have rocks in your head.

Before I was even in the house, the tears started down my cheeks. I got up to our room as fast as I could. Thank goodness Mom wasn't here, so I could cry.

I guess I am more fond of Johnny Vecchio than I realized. *I* should be the one singing that stupid Star Point song: "I Got It Bad and That Ain't Good."

DECEMBER 21, 1941

Dear Diary,

I brought up my shoe and belt problem with Mom today. She said I couldn't get new penny loafers this Christmas because we had to live on peanuts now. Any extra money we have, she wants us to contribute to the Red Cross War Fund. I yelled at her, saying I didn't think I could wait till the war was over. I need friends *now!* She told me I was being crazy. We had a big fight. She said shoes and belts don't make friends. I said in this town they do. She said the girls here were just being snooty and infantile, and I shouldn't take it all so seriously. I shouted, "Yes, I know they are, but I still want them to like me!" I was all wound up. I cried as I told her I hated the gap between my teeth and I needed a slimmer waistline. All she said was, "Phooey." That sent me around the bend. "It's not phooey! It's not!" I said. Again she accused me of being crazy, and I know I am, but I can't help it.

DECEMBER 22, 1941

Dear Diary,

It was a lonely afternoon with Mom volunteering at the church all day.

After supper, all I could think about was that the stupid Christmas dance was taking place at that very moment. I made hot chocolate for myself in the kitchen. Clara was finishing the dishes, so I offered her a cup, too. She accepted, and we sat together in front of the fire in the parlor.

I found myself telling her all about Maxine and the Star Points, and Johnny and the dance tonight, and about how I felt left out of everything.

She listened gravely. She said she knew just what I meant. She said that when she was twelve, the German government wouldn't allow her to go to school with German children anymore because she was Jewish. She said all her neighbors stopped speaking to her family.

I was shocked. What a horrible thing to happen to somebody! I felt worse than ever, so spoiled and selfish.

All I could think to say was something stupid like, "My problems are so tiny compared with yours."

I wanted to ask her more questions about what had happened to her in Germany, but just then her mother called her.

After she went upstairs, I sat alone, listening to the distant waves and the whistling wind. I shivered as I tried to imagine Clara's life in Germany.

The sound of the ocean pounding at night on a dark shore gives me such a sad feeling, like I'm listening to the very heart of loneliness.

DECEMBER 23, 1941

Dear Diary,

I told Mom what Clara had told me, and she was very touched. Even though she's trying to save money, she gave me fifty cents so Clara and I could see *Citizen Kane* and have sodas after.

I loved *Citizen Kane*. Over our vanilla sodas at the drugstore, I tried to explain to her why Mr. Kane, one of the richest men on earth, longed for his childhood sled on his deathbed. I said it was because little things often mean so much more than big things.

Clara shook her head. "Sometimes evil people can kill even the beauty in little things," she said.

"Did evil people ever try to hurt you?" I asked her.

She nodded, then said evil people had once come into her house.

I figured she wanted to tell me her story. So I casually asked, "What did the evil people do?"

Clara just stared at me, looking terribly sad. I felt like I'd opened the door to her worst memories.

"I'm sorry," I said, feeling guilty and remembering Mom's warning not to pry. If Clara wanted to tell me something this personal she would tell me in her own way and in her own time.

I tried to blow away the clouds by changing the subject to Theo. I said I thought he might like seeing *Citizen Kane*, too.

Clara's face brightened at once. "No, that crazy man likes only to work," she said. She told me Theo has been working since he was twelve years old, when his father died. Even though he hurt his leg a few years ago in a fishing accident, he still works night and day to help out his mother.

Clara's eyes were shining the whole time she talked about Theo. You can tell she's crazy about him. I'm glad there is something in her life now that makes her happy.

DECEMBER 24, 1941

Dear Diary,

Christmas Eve. After Mom and I went to a candlelight service at church, she gave me my Christmas gifts: a white belt and pair of penny loafers. I was shocked. I told her that I thought we weren't supposed to give presents this year and that I didn't have a thing for her. She hugged me and said that just having me with her was the greatest gift. Her kindness made me burst into tears.

DECEMBER 25, 1941

Dear Diary,

Merry Christmas.

Mrs. Hawkins and Mrs. Rosenthal are both in bed

with bad colds, and Miss Burke spent the day at her sister's. So Theo, Clara, Mom, and I were the only ones at dinner. With just the four of us, I took notice of how gently Theo speaks to Clara, and how she stares at him with loving eyes.

After dinner, I went into the kitchen and caught them kissing!

It makes me happy to see Theo and Clara together. They're quite alike in some ways. They both were forced to grow up fast.

DECEMBER 27, 1941

Dear Diary,

Clara tapped on my door after lunch today and asked if I wanted to go to the ten-cent store with her and Theo.

"Whoopee," I said. I had been feeling bored stiff.

The three of us walked through a wet, windy snow. As soon as we stepped inside the store, we ran into the Vecchio family — Johnny, Bill, and their parents!

Johnny was all smiles. "This is Maddie Beck, Dad," he said. "The girl with the dad in the navy. She knows all about war stuff."

I nodded. Suddenly Clara took my arm and said, "Maddie, you must hurry now and prepare for your date!"

"Oh, yes! Bye!" I called to Johnny.

We grabbed Theo and hurried out of the store. On the street, Clara and I cracked up laughing.

"That was good, no?" she said — except she says "good" like "goooot."

"Very goooot!" I said, making Theo laugh, too.

DECEMBER 29, 1941

Dear Diary,

A storm's coming. A hard, cold wind is blowing, making the windows rattle. Clara and Mom both have colds now, so they stayed away from dinner, along with Mrs. Rosenthal and Mrs. Hawkins. That left just me, Miss Burke, and Theo to slurp our cod soup together.

While we were at the table, Miss Burke wondered aloud why the newspapers no longer print daily weather reports.

"They don't want to aid the enemy," Theo muttered.

I asked him what he meant, and he said that our weather reports would let any German U-boats close to our shore know when the sea was going to be calm or stormy, helping them make their plans.

Theo's words seemed to roll right off Miss Burke, but they gave me a jolt. German U-boats close to our shore? I have to talk to him about this, as soon as I can catch him alone.

DECEMBER 30, 1941

Dear Diary,

The wind's still blowing hard. It feels like it's blowing right through me as I sit here, feeling scared.

Theo came home from the harbor after dark, smelling of fog and fish. I followed him out into the laundry room. As he pulled off his ice-caked mitts and waders, I asked him if he thought there were any Nazi U-boats off the coast of Long Island.

He said yep, that the U-boats are creeping up and down the East Coast like water snakes.

I asked him how they got here from so far away. He explained that they can glide thousands of miles under-sea without being seen. He knows some fishermen who work for the Coast Guard, and they told him they've been helping patrol the waters with minesweepers, looking for explosives planted by the Nazis.

I was dumbstruck. Theo asked me not to say anything about the U-boats around Mrs. Rosenthal, because she's scared enough of the Germans as it is.

I told him of course I wouldn't. Why, I won't even tell Mom, for that matter. It might worry the heck out of her, too.

There's only one person I'd like to share this information with. But he doesn't deserve to know it.

JANUARY 1, 1942

Dear Diary,
I have two New Year's resolutions:

1. Write to Dad a lot and let him know how much I love him.
2. Be a friend to Clara Rosenthal and other persecuted peoples wherever I find them.

President Roosevelt proclaimed today a national day of prayer, to ask for God's help in the days to come. He also signed the Declaration of United Nations, which affirms the alliance of the United States and twenty-five Allied nations to fight Germany and Axis countries.

Time magazine has named President Roosevelt "Man of the Year." The magazine said that Roosevelt once told the people of this country their generation would have a "rendezvous with destiny." He was right, the magazine says. The United States now stands for the hopes of the world.

A rendezvous with destiny — those might be the most beautiful, dramatic words I've ever heard put together. I'd like to personally have a rendezvous with destiny. I'd like to meet destiny alone on a dark path and fight for the good. I only wish I had someone to share my fight with me.

JANUARY 5, 1942

Dear Diary,

First day back at school. I managed to be calm and cool. Johnny spoke to me a couple of times but I barely answered him. When he waved at me from his lunch table, I ignored him completely.

Maxine and the Star Points seem as snooty in 1942 as they did in 1941.

JANUARY 6, 1942

Tonight, as Mom and I wrote letters to Dad, our radio show was interrupted by war news. The announcer said that Manila, the capital of the Philippines, fell to the Japs yesterday. Mom and I listened silently as Eleanor Roosevelt came on the air and said that the war was on a vaster scale than anything we had ever dreamed of before.

Mom and I didn't look at each other or say a word. I knew we were both wondering the same thing: What does all this mean for Dad?

JANUARY 7, 1942

Dear Diary,

Hard rain all day. Mr. O'Malley asked me to scan the newspaper and find something important to share with the class.

I reported that Mrs. Roosevelt had expressed concern about employers firing foreign-born citizens.

Mrs. Roosevelt warns us to beware of Nazi techniques: "Pit race against race, religion against religion, prejudice against prejudice. Divide and conquer! We must not let that happen here."

The class seemed impressed with Mrs. Roosevelt's words. Some kids had questions. I called on everyone who raised their hand, except Johnny, of course. I'm sure he's aware that I'm giving him the cold shoulder, but I don't think he's figured out why.

JANUARY 8, 1942

Dear Diary,

Every day now at 6 P.M., church bells ring all over town. They ring to remind people to stop what they're doing and pray for one minute for God's help to win the war.

When the bells ring, everyone at our table bows their heads. During our silent minute, I feel very close to Clara, Mrs. Rosenthal, Theo, Mrs. Hawkins, Miss Burke, and my mom. It's as if we're all sending up one prayer, a sort of family prayer to God.

JANUARY 9, 1942

Dear Diary,

Miracles happen.

On the way home from school, Johnny rode up alongside my bike. He didn't say a thing, and neither did I. It was awkward, but fascinating because he kept riding alongside me all the way home.

When I pulled into our driveway, he pulled in, too. "Hey, why are you sore at me?" he said.

"I'm not sore," I said.

"Oh, I thought you were sore," he said.

"Why should I be sore?" I asked.

He shrugged.

There was silence for a moment. Then he started to turn his bike around. I saw that I was about to lose my chance to speak my mind. Instead of pouring forth with a tirade, though, I simply said, "Did you have a good time at the Christmas dance?"

His face broke into one of his best grins. "Oh, is *that* why you're sore?" he asked.

I repeated that I wasn't sore, but doggone it, I could feel my face turning as red as an apple.

Johnny just kept grinning. He said he *had* to go to the dance with Maxine. His mom made him because his dad works for her uncle.

I laughed — I couldn't help it. I blurted out joyfully, "Did you know there are German U-boats off Long Island?"

His eyes got huge. I told him all about the Coast Guard and the minesweepers. He said we should ride along the shore together and check it out as soon as possible. He also said I should come over and see his map. He told me he's added red flags to the Pacific, showing the places the Japanese have taken over: Wake Island, Guam, Hong Kong, and Manila.

When I got inside, I tapped on Clara's door and told her Johnny and I were pals again.

"Whoopee," she said with a smile.

JANUARY 10, 1942

Dear Diary,

Good things happen in bunches. A letter from Dad today. He loved our Christmas package. He read one of the James M. Cain detective books in just a couple of hours. He'd blown his nose on the handkerchiefs, eaten our treats, memorized our love notes, and kissed nobody (underlined two times) under the mistletoe. He's a riot. He sounded real cheerful, and that made us cheerful. Mom and I even danced together as the Harry James Orchestra played "You Made Me Love You" on the radio.

JANUARY 13, 1942

Dear Diary,

I nearly had a heart attack today! Johnny and I took a bike ride along the beach after school. I didn't really expect to see anything. But then we *did* see something! We saw this huge black shiny thing in the water! It floated up above the surface and then disappeared.

We waited for it to reappear. My heart pounded like I was going to have a heart attack. But the black thing never came back.

I shouted above the wind that we should tell Theo. We rode home so fast, my bicycle chain popped off and I had to push my bike the rest of the way.

Fortunately we didn't have to search long for Theo. Just as we got to the house, we saw him coming down the street with his ice-fishing gear. Together we told him about what we'd seen, and he nodded, looking thoughtful. Then he said, "I think what you two saw was a whale. A humpback, maybe. One's been spotted near here lately."

"A whale. Jeepers," said Johnny.

"Just a whale?" I said.

I felt a little foolish. But Theo didn't act like I was a dope. The fact is, Theo always treats me with respect, like I'm his equal, actually, and not just a kid.

JANUARY 15, 1942

Dear Diary,

Today, in the library at school, I saw a photograph in *Newsweek* that made me gasp. It was a photo of six servicemen on the deck of an aircraft carrier in the Pacific.

Though the men were in dark silhouette, one of them looked just like Dad! He was leaning against the ship railing exactly the same way Dad is in the photo beside my bed. "I think that's my dad!" I said, and a group gathered around me, including Maxine.

She had a tender look in her eyes as she studied the

photo. She then looked at me with the same caring expression. "Tell your dad we're all rooting for him, Maddie," she said.

I have to admit that was a really nice thing for her to say — especially since it's been obvious lately that Johnny Vecchio is more mine than hers.

JANUARY 16, 1942

Dear Diary,

Unbelievable top secret information from Theo today! He told me and Johnny that one of his Coast Guard friends confided in him that the Coast Guard had picked up a German radio message. They heard a voice with an accent say, "You escape this time. Next time we sink you. *Heil* Hitler."

Theo explained that the voice must have come from a U-boat right off *our* shore! Probably the Germans had tried to torpedo a merchant ship traveling through the shipping lanes out of New York harbor.

Then Theo said the *most* shocking thing:

"Word is, a German invasion fleet might be coming to our coast at any time." Then he limped inside.

Johnny and I just stared at each other in shock. We couldn't even get out the word "jeepers."

Finally I took a deep breath and told Johnny we shouldn't tell anyone, not even his brother, Bill. We don't want people to panic.

Johnny agreed. He said we should start regular beach patrols. I said yeah, every day after school we should ride our bikes along the shore and look for periscopes sticking up out of the water.

We decided that when the two of us couldn't patrol together, we'd write our findings in a note and leave it in this hollow stump we pass on the way to school, like secret agents. In fact, we even have a code — we write two letters past the correct alphabet letter. Example: for "a," we write "c."

I'd better write a letter to Dad now. But you can bet I'm not going to worry him with this stuff. It's odd, but I may end up seeing more enemy action than he sees.

JANUARY 18, 1942

Dear Diary,

Johnny had to baby-sit today, so I patrolled the beach alone, looking for signs of an invasion fleet. I rode against the wind from the Coast Guard station all the way down to the three big dunes.

Once I screeched on my brakes because I thought I saw a periscope sticking up, but it turned out to be just a piece of wood. Another time, I saw something long and brown tumbling through the waves, but it turned out to be a piece of wood, too.

My hands were almost frozen by the time I left a note for Johnny in the hollow stump.

It said: Vyq cngtvu, hcnug cnctou, pq cevkqp vcmgp. (Two alerts, false alarms, no action taken.)

JANUARY 20, 1942

Dear Diary,

Still no sign of the invasion fleet. But today the local paper confirmed definite U-boat activity near here. It says on January 14, a Norwegian tanker was torpedoed and sank just sixty miles southeast of Montauk Point by a German U-boat! "The sinking has revealed the close presence of German submarines to the shoreline of the United States."

Now everybody knows. Not just me, Johnny, and Theo. Theo still doesn't want the Rosenthals to know, however. When he showed the article to me, he said I could borrow the paper, but I shouldn't let Clara and her mother see it.

I carried the paper over to Johnny's house to show him. He said our patrols are really important. I agreed. *Really* important. Heck, we might have prevented this if the U-boat had come a little closer to shore and we'd reported it in time. I wonder if the "false alarms" I saw yesterday were actually wreckage from the tanker.

JANUARY 23, 1942

Dear Diary,

Johnny and I were discussing the torpedoing of the tanker today when Clara stepped out onto the porch. I punched Johnny's arm and shook my head. He shut up like a clam. I'm sure Clara noticed, because she looked embarrassed and went right back inside.

Doggone it, what if she thought we were talking about Jews or something? I can't bear to think that we might have hurt Clara's feelings.

JANUARY 24, 1942

Dear Diary,

Tonight I knocked on Clara's door and invited her to come listen to Benny Goodman. She said she had to stay in because her mother wasn't well. I was afraid she might be telling a white lie, so I blurted out I was sorry if I hurt her feelings yesterday. I told her that Johnny and I were only playing a game. We didn't mean to shut her out.

She just smiled and said her feelings hadn't been hurt. She said she thought Johnny might have been saying sweet, romantic things to me.

I quickly told her that our relationship wasn't like that. He and I are just best pals, I told her. I love it that way.

Clara smiled as if she only half-believed me.

But it's true! When you're just best pals with someone,

you can be completely yourself. You don't need to wear green velvet jumpers and peppermint-pink blouses. You can smile without worrying about the gap between your teeth.

JANUARY 28, 1942

Dear Diary,

Mom and I have both been so busy lately, we hardly see each other. While I'm patrolling the shore with Johnny, she's raising money for the Red Cross War Fund, and helping organize their blood drive. She's also heading up the Free Library's book drive to gather books for servicemen.

I imagine next she'll try to get a job at a defense plant! I just read that thirty thousand women are already working in the plants, making parachutes and gas masks.

Sometimes I think Mom keeps herself extra busy so she won't worry so much about Dad. I don't know why she's so worried though. He's promised us he was not (underlined three times) in harm's way.

FEBRUARY 2, 1942

Dear Diary,

A letter from Dad today. He said he'd finished the rest of the books we'd sent him. He asked for more. What a coincidence! Now that Mom's running the book drive for servicemen, she can pick out the best books and send them straight to Dad. I can just hear what he'll say: "It pays to know people in high places."

FEBRUARY 9, 1942

Dear Diary,

Several times lately I've caught Mom staring anxiously out the window at the distant ocean. I know she's not thinking about a German invasion fleet. She's thinking about Dad. It's as if she's hoping his ship will appear over the horizon at any moment, bringing him home to us. If she catches me looking at her, she smiles sadly. I just smile back, afraid to pry.

A little while ago, Theo came back late from scouring the bay for scallops. In secret, he told me he saw a flare out at sea as he was walking home in the dark. He's afraid it might have been an enemy signal, and he's going to report it to the Coast Guard tomorrow.

I'm huddled in a blanket near our drafty window right now, watching the sky for strange lights. If it weren't so dark and cold, I'd dash to Johnny's house before Mom gets home and tell him about Theo's sighting.

Johnny's been calling me "Mad" lately. I like that. Mad Beck. Or how about Mad Vecchio? Gee, I'm crazy, I don't want to marry him. Like I told Clara, I love just being his best pal. I do, darn it.

FEBRUARY 10, 1942

Dear Diary,

Theo said the Coast Guard told him the flare he thought he saw last night was just a falling star. He doesn't know whether to believe them or not. The good news is that tomorrow Theo is going to start courses to be part of the county volunteer Civil Defense Force. He said it's sort of a "home front army" that protects Americans in case the enemy action reaches our shores.

"We'll lick those monsters," he said, putting his hand

over Clara's at dinner. I get the feeling Theo would fight the whole German army by himself for Clara's sake. It's a shame his bad leg keeps him out of the military.

FEBRUARY 11, 1942

Dear Diary,

When Theo came home this afternoon, he told us about his day at the Civil Defense Force's training course. At the fairgrounds, the New York State Troopers staged a demonstration of defense against chemical warfare. The volunteers even got to put on masks and enter a tent full of tear gas!

Once Theo has completed the training, he can choose to be an air-raid warden, a medical helper, a messenger, or a member of a road repair squad — or even a bomb squad!

He is so darn lucky. I wish they'd let kids join the Civil Defense Force and be a part of the home front army.

It's not fair.

FEBRUARY 13, 1942

Dear Diary,

A swell idea occurred to me when I woke up this morning. I started thinking that maybe Johnny and I should start a club, a club for kids to help on the home front. It wouldn't be like the Star Points club, where only a privileged few can belong. In my club, any kid who wants to work seriously for the war effort can join. By "kid" I mean six to thirteen years old, so a kid as young as Bill Vecchio could participate.

I can't wait to tell Johnny when I get to school.

LATER

Dear Diary,

Johnny loves, and I mean LOVES my idea of starting a club together. We discussed it all the way home, walking our bikes. Our motto will be: "Victory does not come without a price."

I suggested we use Mrs. Roosevelt's words as our guiding light, the words I have taped to my wall: *"You are going to have a great opportunity. There will be high moments in which your strength and ability will be tested. I have faith in you."*

We're thinking of calling the club Kids Fight for Freedom, or K3F.

We decided we'll announce the club idea at school on Friday after we've had a couple more planning meetings.

FEBRUARY 14, 1942

Dear Diary,

An amazing thing happened late this afternoon. After we coasted on our bikes along the shore, talking about our club, Johnny asked if I'd looked in the tree stump lately. I said no, and he didn't say anything more about it.

After he drove off toward home, I naturally went to look in the tree stump.

Guess what I found.

A piece of notebook paper with a heart drawn on it. Inside the heart, it said: Dg oa xcngpvkpg. (Be my valentine.)

Johnny Vecchio wants *me* to be his valentine?

I scribbled a little valentine note back. I drew a heart and, in the middle of it, I wrote: Qmca. (Okay.) Maybe he'll check the stump after church tomorrow.

What does all this mean? Will I have to change my way of acting around him? Change the way I look and dress?

FEBRUARY 16, 1942

Dear Diary,

Johnny must have found my note, because when he came up to me in the school yard this morning, he winked. Neither of us mentioned the valentines, though. We just leaped into a discussion about the K3F club. What a relief we have the club to talk about. It would have been embarrassing to talk about "us." I feel like Johnny and I have both silently agreed to keep our romantic feelings toward each other a secret. Not just from the world, but a little bit from ourselves, too.

Thank goodness. I don't want to start worrying about my appearance or my behavior when I'm with him. I want to just keep being my old self.

As for K3F club news, Johnny insisted that I should be the "colonel," since it was my idea in the first place. He said he'd be happy to be the "major." All the other kids can be enlisted persons, like "sergeants" or "corporals," depending on their age. But the enlisted kids can become officers by brave deeds and good works.

Tomorrow we're going to figure out just what we mean by "brave deeds" and "good works."

FEBRUARY 17, 1942

Dear Diary,

In my whole life I've never had so much fun. Johnny and I had a meeting today and decided that our K3F club will give kids points for doing these things:

1. Buying Defense Stamps with savings from allowance
2. Giving allowance to the Red Cross War Fund
3. Selling War Bonds to neighbors
4. Collecting used books for servicemen
5. Gathering scrap metal for the county's Salvage for Victory drive and women's silk stockings to be used for parachutes and medical supplies
6. Volunteering to help make first-aid kits for the Red Cross
7. Collecting newspapers and binding them into stacks

We decided not to include U-boat patrol in the list of activities because we don't want to create a panic about the situation. Just the two of us — "Colonel" and "Major" — will patrol the beach.

FEBRUARY 20, 1942

Dear Diary,

Today Johnny and I made our big announcement to the class. When we described the K3F club, kids seemed genuinely knocked out by the idea.

We wrote on the board: "Victory does not come without a price." Under that, we listed our seven ideas of what kids can do for the war effort. This led to a big discussion of what other things they could do.

Bert Lyman suggested that club members make signs to hang around town, inspiring *all* citizens to do the things on our list. (Bert's got a good brain and could easily become one of our first captains.)

Mr. O'Malley said he would talk to the principal about us announcing the club to the whole school in assembly next week. He said we could take a half hour every morning to record the "good works" that kids report to us.

After school, Johnny and I walked our bikes home together so we could talk. Again, neither of us said anything about our valentines. We only talked about the K3F club and a little about my dad. But sometimes Johnny stared at me in a way that made me feel sort of fluttery. I had to fight to feel like a colonel again.

FEBRUARY 22, 1942

Dear Diary,

All weekend, Johnny and I have kept up our planning. Today we sat on my front porch in the cold and made lists of all our ideas. Bill was with us because Johnny had to baby-sit. The little guy kept saying, "Holy smokes" whenever we said something keen.

Mom thinks our club idea is really swell. She served us cookies and hot chocolate while we worked.

We spent a lot of time trying to figure out what will happen when kids collect points for their war effort. We finally decided they should either get promoted or get special insignia. (In my experience, all kids love insignia.) I suggested we could make paper medals. Kids could pin them to their clothes.

When I suggested the idea of a "Medal of Honor" for a kid who makes a ton of points, I thought poor Bill would die. He actually collapsed on the ground and howled with joy.

After Johnny and Bill left, Theo came home with a scary piece of news: A couple of days ago, a Japanese submarine shelled the coast of California. No one was hurt, but it was the first direct attack on American soil in the war. The sub was only a half mile offshore. This is exactly the kind of thing Johnny and I have been trying to prevent from happening here on Long Island.

FEBRUARY 26, 1942

Dear Diary,

This morning, in the special half hour allotted to us, Johnny and I enrolled kids from our class into the K3F club. Maxine and all the Star Points stood in line, eagerly waiting to join up. It almost made me sad to see them acting so humble and eager. I guess my anger toward them is water under the bridge now. Two months ago, who would have ever thought *I'd* soon be running the best club in town?

I have to write Dad a long letter now, telling him all about the club. I can just see him sharing my letter with his buddies, so I'd better make it good.

FEBRUARY 27, 1942

Dear Diary,

Johnny and I gave our assembly presentation today. A funny thing happened before we went onstage. While we were standing in the wings, Johnny took hold of my hand. He gave it a big squeeze. Then he gave me a quick kiss on my cheek and said, "Good luck." The next thing I knew, we were introduced by the principal and went onstage.

I haven't had a real chance to think about that squeeze and kiss until now.

Is the truth starting to creep out into the open? That we're *more* than just best pals?

Stay tuned. . . .

MARCH 2, 1942

Dear Diary,

Quickly, first the Johnny-Maddie News of the Day: We got one check next to the "Best Pals" category, and one check next to the "Romantic" category.

In the "Best Pals" category, we planned more stuff for the club. In the "Romantic" category, he stared fondly at me a few times and, on one occasion, gently brushed a lock of hair off my forehead.

Now, for the War News of the Day:

The radio said that 112,000 Japanese Americans were being forced to move to "assembly centers." Japanese men, women, and children are being forced out of their homes here in the United States. Mom said she doesn't understand why this is necessary. She said it doesn't seem fair. After all, many of these Japanese people were actually born here.

I think she's right. Remember Eleanor Roosevelt's words? I have them written down. She said we should not pit race against race. Religion against religion. Prejudice against prejudice. Divide and conquer — we must not let that happen here, she said.

MARCH 3, 1942

Dear Diary,

This week, the cover of *Newsweek* shows a man wearing a helmet who has his fingers pressed to his lips. It says, "Shhhh. Fight Against Loose Talk . . ." Mom says it means that you're never supposed to talk about things concerning the military. Spies and Nazi sympathizers might be anywhere.

I asked her if that was the reason the government was making Japanese Americans live apart from other Americans.

Mom said she couldn't believe that all of those people were spies. She said little children aren't spies! She thinks it's a tragedy, and someday everyone will see it that way.

MARCH 4, 1942

Dear Diary,

Tonight at dinner, the whole group talked about the K3F club. Miss Burke actually had a very good idea. She said the Masonic Temple had recently started a servicemen's club and they might need furniture and stuff. She said Johnny and I should go by there and talk to them about helping out.

There was a good quote from President Roosevelt in the paper today:

"The months just ahead are the critical months of the war. Victory depends in large measure on the increased war production we are able to get from our factories and arsenals in the spring and summer of 1942. This is total war. We are all under fire — soldiers and civilians alike . . . We are all belligerents. To win we must fight."

Mom read this quote to me a little while ago. She's wondering seriously if she should get a job in a defense factory.

MARCH 5, 1942

Dear Diary,
Johnny, Bert, and I went to see the lady in charge of the servicemen's club today. She seemed delighted and

asked us to please spread the word to the kids that they need all kinds of things. Just minutes ago, I finished making a sign that says:

KIDS FIGHTING FOR FREEDOM IS PUTTING OUT THE CALL! THE SERVICEMEN'S CLUB NEEDS YOUR HELP! CHAIRS AND CHINA! LAMPS AND RUGS! TABLES AND PLATES! FORKS AND SPOONS! PLEASE DELIVER YOUR CONTRIBUTIONS DIRECTLY TO THE MASONIC TEMPLE ON FULTON STREET.

MARCH 7, 1942

Dear Diary,

A heavy snowfall last night. Everything quiet today. Mom, Miss Burke, Clara, and I all knitted in front of the fire.

Mom had a great idea for the K3F club. She suggested we give information to kids on how to plant "Victory Gardens" this spring. That's a garden with everyday foods for a family, like cabbage, cauliflower, carrots, peppers, peas, potatoes, spinach, radishes, tomatoes, and squash.

Mom said Americans need to plant Victory Gardens

so transportation facilities won't have to be used to carry food to grocers and can be used for military purposes instead. Mom even offered to come to the school and talk about all this. I'm thinking that the K3F club should have a series of special guest speakers.

By the way, Miss Burke has come through in a swell way again. She's going to tell the local paper to write an article about us. She has a good connection there — a woman from her church who writes the garden column.

I can't wait to tell Johnny.

MARCH 9, 1942

Dear Diary,

Tonight Theo suggested that K3F members collect bacon grease from their mothers' kitchens so the Civil Defense Force can use the lard to make glycerine for explosives. And he said we should roll up little pieces of tinfoil for collection.

Theo seems impressed with my new leadership role. He calls me "Colonel" and says, "How's it going, Colonel? Win the war today?"

Even though he has a gruff manner, something about Theo is positively sweet. I love the way he brings Clara little gifts from the shore, like a pretty shell or a smooth stone.

I regret I haven't had much time to be a good friend to her lately. But I'm sure she understands.

I've also not written Dad very much lately, but I'm sure he'd understand, too, if he knew how busy I was with the club and all.

MARCH 10, 1942

Dear Diary,

On our U-boat bike patrol today, Johnny pointed at the ocean as if he'd just seen something suspicious. We both stopped our bikes and stood in the windy cold and stared at the whitecaps for a long time. Finally we shrugged and went on our way. It's amazing how Johnny and I can just silently beam our thoughts to each other sometimes.

Oh gee, is this anything like love?

MARCH 12, 1942

Dear Diary,

I had a great idea today. It was inspired by an announcement I read in the paper that said a Russian refugee is going to speak at the Presbyterian Church, giving a firsthand account of the Nazi invasion of Russia.

So my idea is: Clara Rosenthal can be one of K3F's special guest speakers and speak to our school, giving a firsthand account of the persecution of the Jews in Germany. I know she finds it sad to talk about the past. But this would be in service to a higher cause. I feel certain she'll see the importance of trying to educate kids about Hitler's evil.

(I hate to brag, but I think I'm the only one in our school who has a Jewish refugee for a friend.)

MARCH 13, 1942

Dear Diary,
I am such an idiot.
Today after school, I saw Clara and Theo on the porch. I bounded up to them and blurted out my idea

about Clara being a special guest speaker and talking to the school about the Nazis and the Jews.

I knew at once I'd made a mistake. Clara looked upset, and Theo scowled at me.

I quickly muttered that it was a stupid idea and I was sorry. My face felt like it was on fire.

As I started to leave, Clara grabbed my hand. "I'm sorry, Maddie," she said in a soft, sad voice. She said she could not talk about these things yet. Especially in public to so many people. She said maybe someday she could, but not now.

I said I understood. I felt close to tears. I'd rather die than hurt Clara. Maybe her story is simply too sad for her to tell to anyone.

MARCH 14, 1942

Dear Diary,

Mrs. Hawkins was frying bacon tonight. So I brought her a clean, empty can and asked for some fat from the pan. She didn't understand. She said fat wasn't good to eat.

"Not for me! I'm giving fat to the club!" I said, nearly shouting. (Her deafness seems to be getting worse.)

Mrs. Hawkins shook her head in disapproval, but poured the fat into my can, anyway.

Later, at dinner, she told everyone she'd never in her life heard of a fat club. She wanted to know what kind of people joined a fat club.

I cracked up and explained to the others what had happened. They cracked up, too, and soon we were all laughing so hard, we couldn't stop. Though I think she still didn't understand, Mrs. Hawkins joined in because she's such a sweet sport. It was kind of crazy, the way we all howled over this misunderstanding. I think all of us needed a good laugh.

MARCH 16, 1942

Dear Diary,

A letter from Dad today. Big chunks were blacked out. (Where is he? I wonder this all the time.) But the censors didn't cross out the part that said he was so proud of me. He thinks the K3F club is a super idea. He says all his men think so, too. See? I predicted he would share my letter with his buddies. I know him. He also said he'd like to hear from me more often.

MARCH 20, 1942

Dear Diary,

Mom gave blood at the Red Cross today. I got the funniest feeling thinking about it. Her blood might be transfused into some soldier somewhere. He might be in a hospital recovering from a wound. He might be in a foxhole, in a plane, on a ship. Wherever he is, a part of Mom will be with him.

I shared these thoughts with Johnny, and he said it gave him the shivers. He said I should write them down and send them in to the newspaper. He said I was deep. "You're deep, Mad," he said.

I could only sigh and shake my head modestly. But I wonder, *Am* I deep?

MARCH 24, 1942

Dear Diary,

Johnny says Bill got into trouble the other night because he kept going around singing, "Praise the Lord and pass the ammunition," until his mom finally shouted, "Enough!"

Laughing about Bill is one of the things Johnny and I love to do most. We're both crazy about that little guy.

And each other? Today I'd have to say the thermometer reading was high on the sweetheart end. After we stopped laughing, Johnny ran his hand over my cheek. I got chills when he did that.

Oh brother, I want to stop this. Thinking about this kind of thing makes me feel less like a colonel and more like a silly Star Point.

MARCH 26, 1942

Dear Diary,

Japanese troops have attacked our forces in a place called Bataan. In cases like this, I'm glad Dad's on the sea, and not on land. If I had to worry about him fighting on land, I'd be in a state of constant anxiety.

APRIL 1, 1942

Dear Diary,

There's been so much to do, I haven't had time to write in my diary for almost a week. And now, there's more! Mr. O'Malley suggested to Johnny and me that K3F put together an extra calisthenics program (separate from gym) to encourage kids to build up their muscles so we'll have a "sturdier nation." It seems he saw something about this in a magazine.

For crying out loud! Johnny and I can't do everything! I'm thinking this might actually be a job we can give Maxine. She enjoys thinking about her looks so much. As a matter of fact, the other day she asked if she could design a uniform for members of K3F. Positively not, I told her, *this* club is not about clothes and shoes and looks! It's about helping win the war!

She just shrugged and accepted it. It pays to be the commanding officer sometimes.

APRIL 2, 1942

Dear Diary,

Maxine's excited about leading the girls in jumping jacks and sit-ups before school. Bert will lead the boys. Maxine hinted these jobs warranted promotions for her and Bert. "Jeepers, not so fast," said Johnny. "Let's see how you do first."

Theo said the Civil Defense Force is planning a blackout test for April 23. That means we'll have to turn out all our lights at night to protect the shipping lanes near the Long Island coastline from enemy submarines. Apparently when the lights are on, the Germans can spot our ships at a distance of up to forty-five miles from shore.

Johnny told me lately he's added more Japanese flags to his world map: Papua and New Guinea, the Solomon Islands, Burma, and all of Borneo. The biggest fight now is over the Philippines.

APRIL 4, 1942

Dear Diary,

We haven't heard from Dad in a while. But then I haven't written him in a while, either. I have to buckle down and give him a report on all our club activities.

Gee, I wonder where he is. Mom doesn't like even to speculate. She says the less we know, the better we'll sleep. As long as we don't get a telegram, we don't have to worry, she says.

Never has anything seemed so horrible and wretched

as getting a telegram. If I ever see a telegram boy at our door, I'm afraid I'll start screaming and never stop.

APRIL 6, 1942

Dear Diary,
Last night Theo told me the Civil Defense Force would be having a practice drill on the beach today. So Johnny and I snuck down there to watch. We hid behind a dune and, in the cold, gray weather, we saw a group of men creeping across the sand, pretending to be invaders from an enemy submarine. Suddenly another group dressed as armed police appeared on the beach and opened fire with blank bullets.

It was so scary, I have to confess I actually started to shake. What kind of colonel am I? I fear I'm a complete impostor.

APRIL 11, 1942

Dear Diary,
Something very romantic happened today.
It happened after Johnny and I had our meeting with

the chairman of the county war board. We'd gone to his house to discuss different ways kids can help with the scrap drive.

The chairman said mills are hungry for iron and steel scraps to make ships, tanks, and planes. They need more copper, brass, and other metals. They need rubber, too, from old tires.

"To win this war, the mills need all the scrap left lying around in people's yards — old tools and farm equipment!" he said. "Our war machine is starving for scrap to be melted down!"

The poor guy got so worked up, his face turned beet red. "Tell your friends! Collect scrap to slap a Jap!" he cried.

Johnny and I muffled our laughter until we left the house. Then we started laughing and couldn't stop. We were leaning against the back of the house in the twilight, shaking with laughter — when suddenly Johnny kissed me.

I was so surprised, I said, "Hey!"

"Sorry," he said.

"No, no, 'hey' means 'good,'" I said.

He asked if I was sore.

"Are you kidding?" I told him I was happy.

He said he was happy, too. Then, without another word, we got on our bikes and took off together.

That kiss must mean we are *officially* more than pals now.

J. V. + M. B.

Should I write that on my notebook?

APRIL 13, 1942

Dear Diary,

Miss Burke's connection at the paper seems to have paid off. A reporter wants to interview me and Johnny and take our picture a week from Wednesday. As Dad would say, "It pays to know people in high places."

Speaking of Dad, as soon as I get a copy of the paper with my picture, I'll send him one. The article will floor him. Plus, it'll help him understand why I've been too busy to write him lately.

(I won't say anything about Johnny being my boy-friend, of course. I don't want to make him jealous.)

APRIL 14, 1942

Dear Diary,

This week the paper said that there's a great shortage of ships right now. This shortage is making it very hard for the United States to deliver arms and munitions overseas.

For Mom, this article was the straw that broke the camel's back. She went and got a job as a welder in a defense plant about ten miles from here. She'll get picked up by a friend in the afternoon and return after midnight. She's asked Miss Burke and Mrs. Hawkins to keep an eye on me and make sure I eat a good supper and get my homework done.

The truth is, I'm so busy, I don't really mind. I have the feeling Mom and I are doing the same thing. We think if we work hard enough for the war effort, Dad will be safe and sound. In other words, everything we do, we do for him. He's our shining light. Our beloved. I guess people all over America are going through the same thing. For most people, the war comes down to one special serviceman you desperately love. A father, a brother, a son.

APRIL 18, 1942

Dear Diary,

Beautiful, warm day. Another Civil Defense drill tomorrow. Theo has invited me, Johnny, and Clara to participate. He told Clara he wants her to know that people here will fight the Germans if they ever try to invade us. We will never let the enemy hurt the Jews who live in America, he said.

When he said that, I got the chills. I can't imagine living in a country that would allow anyone to hurt Clara Rosenthal.

APRIL 19, 1942

Dear Diary,

It may sound strange, but Theo, Clara, Johnny, and I had a ball at the Civil Defense drill today.

At a fake bombing site, Clara and I were supposed to pretend to be casualties of a bombing. Theo and Johnny had to get us to the safety of the settlement house, where a fake emergency hospital had been set up.

At first, I was worried that Clara might find the whole

thing upsetting, but my fears were for nothing. Johnny and Theo were so funny trying to rescue us that Clara and I spent more time laughing than anything else. When they tried to carry us out of an old shack that was supposedly "bombed," they dropped me! Then Clara pretended to have a broken leg — and they put the splint on the wrong leg!

We laughed till tears came down our cheeks. I'll admit I never had so much fun.

Afterward, the four of us walked along the sunlit shore. It felt like a double date. Theo and Clara held hands as Theo talked about shad and bluefish. Johnny and I held hands, too, and kept our eyes pinned on the waves for periscopes. Several times we poked one another, but what we saw always turned out to be a seabird or piece of driftwood.

Gee, one thing's for sure: Life's never dull anymore. I'm having a great time. Can a person be in love with the excitement of war? Or is that too wicked?

APRIL 21, 1942

Dear Diary,

It might be time to promote Bill Vecchio from corporal to sergeant. Maybe even give him a medal. On Saturday, in a light spring rain, he drove his uncle's pony cart up and down his street, collecting flattened tin cans for the scrap drive. The tin will be melted down and reused for the war. All the time, he sang in his little high voice Bing Crosby's song "Junk Ain't No Junk No More." He threw his own tin soldiers and roller skates onto the heap.

Bill's already collected so many chewing gum wrappers that he's got a ball of aluminum the size of a baseball. Holy smokes, Bill!

He may be no bigger than a minute, but he's got the heart of a hero.

APRIL 22, 1942

Dear Diary,

Hey, Johnny and I had our picture taken today for the local paper! The photographer included Bill in the picture, too, with his pony cart and his scrap collection, as well as his aluminum baseball.

We're all famous! But I guess you could say there's still miles to go before we sleep.

In fact, Theo now thinks that K3F members should help the Aircraft Watch Service watch the sky for German planes. He's going to draw some pictures of the planes for us to pass around.

APRIL 23, 1942

Dear Diary,

Johnny and I worked as volunteer sky-watchers today, which means we watched the sky for two hours, detailing the number and kinds of planes we saw.

We didn't actually see any, but we did hold hands the whole time. I kept shivering, and I couldn't tell if it was from the cool ocean breeze or from my nerves.

We watched until twilight, when the Coast Guard told us to leave. The beach is strictly off-limits to all civilians after dark.

APRIL 24, 1942

Dear Diary,

Last night we had the first county blackout. It began at 9 P.M. with a five-minute blast of police sirens. Everyone on the road had to pull over and turn their lights out. House lights, streetlights, and traffic lights had to be turned off, too.

Mom stayed home from work because of the blackout. We all gathered in the parlor, except for Theo, who had to help patrol the area. Mom explained as best she could what was going on. Clara tried to translate for her mother. But when all the lights went out, we could hear Mrs. Rosenthal whimper with fear. Clara, Miss Burke, Mrs. Hawkins, Mom, and I all tried to comfort her, like we'd comfort a child afraid of the dark. We said silly things. We laughed. We sang. Mrs. Hawkins even lit a tiny candle and then brought out a surprise for us. A blueberry pie! It was actually delicious! By flickering candlelight, she cut big pieces for each of us, and we all greedily ate the berries and soft crust. Before our tiny light went out, I saw a childlike smile on Mrs. Rosenthal's tear-streaked face.

The blackout lasted three hours. During that time, Mrs. Rosenthal, Mrs. Hawkins, Clara, and Miss Burke all went to sleep sitting on chairs or on the sofa. In the end, only Mom and I were still awake.

Looking out the window, Mom said, "I've never seen such blackness before."

Not even the stars or moon were shining.

APRIL 29, 1942

Dear Diary,

Our picture came out in the paper today! Mr. O'Malley pinned it to the classroom wall. Mom bought ten copies to take to work and church. Of course, we also sent one to Dad right away. I can't wait to hear what he thinks about it.

APRIL 30, 1942

Dear Diary,

National registration for sugar rationing books took place at school today. Sugar has to be rationed now because the ships that deliver it from the Caribbean have to be used to fight the war.

Mom volunteered to register for everyone living in Mrs. Hawkins's Mansion-by-the-Sea. She had to tell the number of pounds of white or brown sugar already owned by our "family unit."

By this simple act of registration, me, Mom, Theo, Mrs. Hawkins, Clara, her mother, and Miss Burke all became members of a family unit. We do feel like a family these days. The war has a weird way of bringing strangers together.

MAY 5, 1942

Dear Diary,

Today Theo came home, wearing an official armband of the Civil Defense Force. Golly, it looks keen.

I'm thinking Johnny and I should consider making armbands for the officers of the K3F (which is still just the two of us). Maxine and Bert might get promoted soon, though. They're actually working quite hard leading the kids in calisthenics every morning. Maxine's invented a cheer that goes, "Pep! Pep! Pep up for the war!"

MAY 8, 1942

Dear Diary,

A great letter from Dad today.

He hasn't gotten my newspaper picture yet, of course. I'll be relieved when he gets it, because once again he mentioned that he'd like to hear more from me. He wondered how the K3F club was doing. He said President and Mrs. Roosevelt would be proud of us.

(Hey, an idea: I'll send one of the newspaper pictures to Mrs. Roosevelt! Our club's doing exactly what she wants kids to do.)

Dad teased Mom about working in the defense plant, but he said he admired her more than ever. He said she was working harder than he was.

He said he was still bored. (Good news.) He's gotten to be a darn good poker player, but he'd give up his poker winnings any day to see our faces. He said he dreams about us a lot.

Good night, sweet Dad.

MAY 9, 1942

Dear Diary

Great war news. A really long headline in *The New York Times* declared what happened yesterday:

JAPANESE REPULSED IN GREAT PACIFIC BATTLE WITH 17 TO 22 OF THEIR SHIPS SUNK OR CRIPPLED AND ENEMY IN FLIGHT PURSUED BY WARSHIPS

I read the article a bit anxiously, wondering if Dad might have been involved in the battle. But I breathed a sigh of relief when I came to "United Nations losses were said to have been comparatively light."

Later, when I showed the article to Johnny, I told him I thought Dad had probably been involved in this victorious Pacific battle. He looked at me in awe and said, "That's really keen, Mad." It's probably awful of me, but I liked getting credit for Dad's service and courage. (In other words, it pays to know people in high places.)

I can't wait to get a letter from Dad and find out what he thinks of my picture in the paper.

MAY 11, 1942

Dear Diary,

I have a terrible spring cold. I keep blowing my nose and can hardly breathe, so Mom wanted me to stay home from school today. I'll probably stay home again tomorrow, but I'm not loafing around. Today, when I had the strength, I worked on a design for a club uniform. I know I told Maxine "positively not," but I'm rethinking my position. Maybe it's not such a bad idea. What about just a simple white blouse or shirt and blue skirt or blue trousers? Any kid could come up with that, couldn't they? An armband would look really keen with that outfit. Maybe the Star Points could embroider a "V" for victory on all the shirt pockets.

MAY 13, 1942

Dear Diary,

Yesterday a telegram came.

Late in the afternoon. Mom was at work. I was sitting in the parlor designing our club uniform, when the front bell rang. I looked out the window and saw the telegram boy at the door.

I started to scream as I always thought I would. I screamed and screamed and I even tried to lock the front door.

Theo limped into the hall and grabbed me and held me, and Miss Burke opened the door and signed for the telegram. It was from the Department of the Navy.

I was shaking and crying as Theo held me. Clara, Mrs. Rosenthal, and Mrs. Hawkins all listened gravely as Miss Burke read the telegram aloud:

THE NAVY REGRETS TO INFORM YOU THAT YOUR HUSBAND LIEUTENANT COMMANDER DAVID BECK HAS BEEN CRITICALLY WOUNDED STOP WE WILL FURNISH MORE DETAILS WHEN AVAILABLE STOP

That's all it said.

They helped me up the stairs to my room, and Mrs. Hawkins and Miss Burke put cold cloths on my face and tried to calm me because I was shaking and sobbing uncontrollably.

Clara stayed and sat with me and, as I cried, she stroked my hair.

Theo drove his truck to Bridgetown to pick up Mom at the defense plant.

By the time they got home, Mom had known the news for some time, but had not spent all her tears. She got into bed with me, and we held each other for a long time, crying our hearts out. When you think you can't cry anymore, you always can.

MAY 14, 1942

Dear Diary,

I didn't go to school today. Miss Burke knows Mr. O'Malley, so she said she'd tell him my situation.

I don't feel like getting out of bed. I just keep staring at the wall, lost in my questions and worries. Clara brought me lunch and supper, but I don't feel like eating or talking. Mom went back to work because she said she doesn't know what else to do. It's better not to have her here, because every time I look at her, I see her sadness and it makes me feel worse. I just want to be alone.

I keep wondering, was Dad flying when he got

wounded? Was he in a battle? Did a torpedo hit his ship? Was he playing poker? Was he writing to us? Was he sleeping? Did he have time to think? Did he lose an eye or a leg? Is he already dead? What exactly did the telegram mean when it said he was "critically wounded"?

I looked up "critically" in the dictionary and all I could find was that it's the adverb of "critical," meaning "crisis" or "turning point."

MAY 16, 1942

Dear Diary,

Yesterday, Mr. O'Malley told the class about my dad. Johnny came by the house, but I told Clara to tell him that I didn't want to see anybody right now.

"Not even Johnny?" she asked in her soft voice.

I shook my head.

No, not Johnny. Especially not Johnny.

I can't be strong now or excited about the K3F club. I just want to be alone and think things through.

I can't get the picture out of my mind of the telegram boy at our door. I've relived that moment a hundred thousand times, as if by reliving it, I can change it, I can undo it, I can make the boy disappear and the day will stay simple and happy forever.

But I know that I'd have to reverse much more than just the boy's telegram. . . . I'd have to go back to some earlier day when Dad got wounded. A day and an hour I don't know a thing about. His last letter was sent May 3. Sometime between then and probably May 10 or 11, he was wounded. Was it May 8? In that victorious battle that made such huge headlines? I feel so guilty now about bragging to Johnny that Dad was probably in that battle.

When I looked at my last words in my May 8 diary entry, I burst into fresh tears. I'd written: "Good night, sweet Dad."

MAY 17, 1942

Dear Diary,

I took a walk on the beach with Mom today. Neither of us said much. I think we're both afraid to burden the other with our grief and worry.

We saw Johnny and Bill sitting on the pilings of the abandoned pier, watching for planes. Johnny saw me and shouted. But I just gave a little wave and kept walking.

When we got home, Mom prepared a covered dish for dinner at the church. She had to take a sugarless dessert, called a "war recipe." I went up to our room while she whipped up a fruit salad.

In spite of her sadness, she keeps going. I don't know how she does it. Just a week ago I would have loved to spot planes with Johnny and Bill. I would have gotten a kick out of helping Mom come up with a war recipe. But now I positively hate war. Everything about it makes me sick.

MAY 18, 1942

Dear Diary,

Mom said I have to go back to school tomorrow. She doesn't want me to sit by the window another day, just moping and biting my nails. I said I'd go, but if any more telegrams or letters, good or bad, arrive about Dad's condition, someone from the house has to come immediately to the school to get me.

It seems cruel beyond words that the navy doesn't tell families more. Loved ones could go insane trying to piece together the story on their own. I cut out a *New York Times* map about the Battle of the Coral Sea, that victorious battle on May 8.

The map shows where Japanese and American ships met near these islands in the Southwest Pacific. I also cut out a *Newsweek* cover concerning that same battle. It shows a stream of American ships and planes with the caption "Thunder at Sea: The Navy Meets the Enemy."

I feel if I stare long and hard enough at these puzzle pieces, maybe they'll reveal Dad's fate somehow.

MAY 19, 1942

Dear Diary,

Today when I went back to school, everyone was extra nice. Maxine and all the Star Points told me they were sorry. Johnny kept trying to catch my eye, but I wouldn't give it to him.

I'm mad at him. I'm not sure why, but it might be because while Dad was in mortal danger, Johnny and I were acting like we were having a ball. Flying around on our bikes, looking for U-boats, running the K3F club like it was all a fun game, holding hands while we plane-spotted. Playing war with Johnny kept me from worrying about Dad enough. It kept me from writing to him enough and praying for him enough.

MAY 20, 1942

Dear Diary,

I officially resigned from the club today. I left my resignation in the hollow stump. This time, my note was not written in code. It said simply:

Dear Johnny,

I have to resign as colonel of K3F. It's your job now. Sorry, Maddie

MAY 21, 1942

Dear Diary,

After school Johnny caught up with me on his bike and asked if we'd heard any more about Dad. I shook my head. He asked if I had any ideas about what had happened to Dad. I said no. I told him I was sorry about resigning my post. Then he surprised me by sounding a little angry.

"You should work harder than ever to help service-men like your dad," he said.

His tone made me lose my temper. "Are you trying to tell me what I should do?" I said.

"I just know you shouldn't turn into a chicken, Mad," he said.

"Oh yeah?" I said.

"Yeah!" he said. His usual sparkling eyes looked furious.

"Well, you don't know anything, Johnny Vecchio," I said coldly. I told him he thought that war was just a big game, but it wasn't a game at all. Then I pedaled away as fast as I could.

I know I was acting mean and crazy. But it made me feel good for a moment. It made me feel stronger — until I got home. Then I broke down and sobbed.

MAY 23, 1942

Dear Diary,

I listen to the sound of the ocean at night and I feel that same terrible loneliness I've always felt listening to the waves in the dark. Except now that terrible deep loneliness is connected to my grief about Dad.

MAY 26, 1942

Dear Diary,

It's been two weeks since we got the telegram. Not another word from the navy since. I keep a constant lookout for another telegram. I never stray far from the front porch. I keep watching out the window for that boy on his bike. I'm obsessed with getting another telegram to find out what's happened to Dad.

MAY 27, 1942

Dear Diary,

Theo peeked inside my room tonight. "How ya doin', Colonel?" he asked.

I was just lying on my bed, with a knot in my stomach, staring at the ceiling. I murmured, "Okay," without bothering to tell him I wasn't a colonel anymore.

Theo said his mother was worried because I hadn't come down for dinner. He said my mom would get mad at all of them if I didn't eat.

I just kept looking at the ceiling and told him I wasn't hungry.

He sat on the edge of Mom's bed and said, "Colonel, I got a gut feeling your pop is going to pull through."

He said he had feelings that were seldom wrong . . . he could predict storms, he could predict the amount of fish that the boats would bring in on a summer day.

I asked him if he had predicted that Dad would get wounded in the first place.

He squinted and slowly nodded. "I predicted to myself that you and your ma might run into a hard time, Colonel."

Good prediction, I thought.

He told me other folks in the house had suffered bad times, too. He said Clara and Mrs. Rosenthal had seen things we couldn't imagine in America. He said that four years ago Nazi storm troopers had broken into their house. They beat Clara's father to death right in front of her eyes.

I felt a jolt of horror go through me when Theo said this. Tears started down my face. But he went on calmly. He said Mrs. Rosenthal had not been right in the head ever since, but somehow Clara had found the strength to go on. She had gotten them out of Germany and over to America, where an uncle lived. When the uncle died, they had no more relatives or friends, and very little money. But once again, Clara found the courage to survive. She'd searched everywhere for a place to live, until she'd come upon Theo and his mother. With them, she had made an arrangement to help in the kitchen in exchange for room and board.

Theo said Clara had faced the darkness and she had won the war. The only thing that worries him, though, is that Clara seems to have lost the ability to cry.

As Theo told me all these things, the knot in my stomach tied itself tighter, and I could hardly breathe. Finally I know Clara's story.

Before Theo left, he patted my hair. "Colonel," he said, "you're a tough officer. I know you're going to make it. Before this is all over, you'll know a lot more about yourself, too."

All I know now is that I'm not like Clara. I don't have the courage to face the darkness like her. All I want to do is run away from the darkness.

MAY 29, 1942

Dear Diary,

Every day after school I still sit on the front porch, waiting for either a telegram or a letter.

My worst fear is that the navy has forgotten all about us. They'll never get in touch with us again, and we'll never know what happened to Dad.

JUNE 2, 1942

Dear Diary,

I cry every night when I'm lying in the dark, trying to sleep. I try to cry into my pillow. Usually I've cried myself to sleep before Mom gets home. But sometimes I'm still awake when she comes in and I know she can hear me sniffing, but she doesn't say anything. I know she doesn't want to pry. But sometimes I wish she would.

JUNE 4, 1942

Dear Diary,

It's been over three weeks since we got the telegram. We've had no more word from the navy. And not one word from Dad himself. If he was recovering, he would write us. I know him. If he was conscious at all, he would write. No news is terrible news, and it makes me feel emptier every day.

I remember in third grade I was in a ballet recital and Mom was hosting a luncheon at the officers' wives' club, so Dad had to come see me alone. He sat in the front row, wearing his white navy uniform, and when I came out in a rose-colored tutu for my solo dance, I caught sight of him beaming at me and all the steps my teacher had taught me went right out of my head. So I made up a dance on the spot. I turned and turned and turned and miraculously I never got dizzy. I danced the best I'd ever danced. I felt like a wind chime, and Dad's smile was the wind making me whirl.

All my life I've felt strong under my dad's gaze. Without him on earth, I imagine I'd feel so completely empty, I'd collapse in on myself and die.

JUNE 5, 1942

Dear Diary,

Tonight I did something against the law: I walked on the beach after dark. For security reasons, all persons, except the Coast Guard, are supposed to keep off the beaches from sunset to sunrise. But at about ten o'clock, while Mom was still at work and everyone had gone to their rooms, I heard Clara singing. The sound of her sweet voice nearly tore my heart out of my chest. I remembered Theo's words: Clara had faced the darkness and won the war.

Suddenly *I* wanted to face the darkness. And the darkest place I know is the beach at night.

I threw on my dungarees and a sweater, then snuck out of the house and ran all the way to the dunes, to the very heart of loneliness.

It was low tide. There was no sign of the Coast Guard beach patrol, so I sat on the sand and stared at the moonlight shimmering on the black water. It actually wasn't as lonely and frightening as I always imagined the beach to be at night. Somehow I found it a little comforting . . . the dark shapes of crabs scavenging the seaweed, the swell of the waves rising and washing over the shore.

I sat there shivering until I thought I saw a flashlight at the end of the beach. Then I ran for home.

Now I'm a little worried that I might be losing my mind. I mean, was I crazy to go to the beach tonight?

JUNE 9, 1942

Dear Diary,

Last day of school. What a relief. I won't have to bear the sad looks that come my way whenever the war's discussed. Or listen to Bert and Johnny talk about K3F plans. (Johnny's the colonel now. Bert's the major.)

Today near the bike stand, they were all talking about New York City's war parade. The Civil Defense Force has invited club members to march with them.

Johnny caught me listening and walked over to me. I tried to move away, but he caught my arm and asked if I wanted to go to the parade with them.

I told him no thanks, I hate war parades (not that I've ever been to one before).

But Johnny wouldn't take no for an answer. He said

we could go together on the train and I should just tell my mom we'd be home before dark.

The way he said "home before dark" suddenly made me feel like a little kid and made me miss my dad so terribly that I snapped, "No," again and started off on my bike.

"Chicken!" Johnny called softly behind me.

"You are!" I retorted, and drove off without looking back.

I can't go to a dumb parade when Dad might be dying or already dead somewhere in the Pacific.

JUNE 10, 1942

Dear Diary,

Johnny's wrong. I'm not a chicken. To prove it, I faced the darkness again tonight. After the house grew quiet, I headed down to the lonely beach. I hid behind a dune while a Coast Guard cutter moved along the foggy shore. When it was gone, I wandered down to the edge of the waves. Soon, clouds covered the moon and a thin rain began to fall. So I went home.

JUNE 11, 1942

Dear Diary,

Mom had the night off tonight. After dinner, she and Clara and I sat on the porch together. We talked about the lilacs blooming and about movies and the jitterbug. We never pried into each other's sorrows. We talked as if nothing were wrong in our lives. We talked like normal people, as if none of us had been shredded to pieces by grief.

JUNE 12, 1942

Dear Diary,

Tonight I got caught.

I'm still shaking. I don't understand what happened, really. I was walking on the foggy beach and when I got close to the abandoned pier, I heard voices and saw the shapes of two men near the dunes. I turned back to go home, but one of the men called out and shined a flashlight on me, and I froze like a rabbit.

The man angrily told me to halt and he asked who I

was and where I lived. I told him my name was Madeline Beck and gave him my address. He ordered me to turn around. I did, and he walked up to me in the dark and shined the flashlight right in my eyes. When I started to turn away, he said, "Look straight into this light, Madeline Beck." And I looked into the light, and I was blinded, and he said, "We're the Coast Guard. You did not see us here. You saw nothing."

Then I heard a man call out from the dunes. It sounded like he spoke a foreign language, but I couldn't tell for sure. Another voice told him to shut up.

Then the man with the flashlight told me to go straight home, and not tell anyone what I'd seen or I'd be arrested. He said they were engaged in a secret military operation.

"Your parents would be sad if you are arrested," he said. "Not one word about this, do you understand? Not one word."

I was so scared, I just said, "Yes, sir. I won't tell. I promise." I started walking away very quickly. Then I began running.

As I ran, I thought I heard some kind of engine offshore. I couldn't see a thing through the fog, though. I panicked and ran so fast, I kept slipping and falling. By the time I got home, I was caked with wet sand.

I can't tell anyone what I saw or heard, or I'll be arrested. I can't believe the Coast Guard would arrest a kid, but this is war. The military has to be cold-blooded in times of war.

Gee, Mom would die if she knew I'd been wandering the beach alone in the dark. Now that I think about it, I can't believe the Coast Guard didn't arrest me right there on the spot.

JUNE 13, 1942

Dear Diary,

I'm still in shock from what happened last night. I was so nervous all day, I never left home. I just sat on the front porch and prayed the Coast Guard wouldn't decide to come to the house and arrest me. After all, they know my name and address.

At one point I nearly jumped out of my skin because this black car slowed down in front of the house and a guy in a dark suit seemed to be staring straight at me. But then the car sped up and was gone, and I realized it probably had nothing to do with me or my being caught on the beach. Someone was probably just looking for a room and saw the NO VACANCY sign.

All day, though, I dreaded someone coming to the door, or the phone ringing. If Mom finds out what I did, her calm surface will crack for sure. Maybe she'll even get in trouble, too, for having a daughter who broke the law.

It's times like these I desperately wish Dad were here. He'd make everything all right.

JUNE 15, 1942

Dear Diary,

The last two days I've stayed close to home. I have the weirdest feeling that the Coast Guard really is keeping an eye on me. This afternoon I was loafing on the porch with Miss Burke, Theo, and Clara when a guy in a suit walked by the house. He paused and looked straight at me. He was wearing sunglasses and a fedora, so I couldn't see his face well.

Theo said, "Can I help you?"

Without a word, the guy turned and walked on.

"My, there's some odd characters in town these days," Miss Burke said.

Theo agreed with her. He went on to tell her about some of the strange people he'd seen down by the wharf.

Right now I'm about to jump out of my skin, thinking every sound I hear is the Coast Guard coming to arrest me. I don't know what to do. I feel like praying to Dad to help me.

JUNE 16, 1942

Dear Diary,

I felt a little calmer today. No sign of weird strangers. Still, I didn't sit on the porch, as I was afraid of being too exposed. I sat in my usual window seat, biting my nails and keeping watch for a telegram or letter. I know my nerves are shattered because of Dad. If we would just hear about him, I wouldn't be so afraid. My imagination wouldn't keep running away with me.

After dinner, from my window perch, I heard Theo and Clara talking on the porch swing. Miss Burke, Mrs. Rosenthal, and Mrs. Hawkins sat in rocking chairs, knitting. Mrs. Hawkins has been encouraging Mrs.

Rosenthal to leave her room more often. She even buys yarn for her.

Theo was telling them about the swordfish running off Montauk Point. He said the price would go down to thirty-five cents a pound now. He told her that great schools of mackerel and tuna have been seen offshore, too.

All their talk was such simple, normal talk, but it was music to my ears. My terror about Dad and my terror about what happened on the beach have made plain, ordinary life seem precious now.

JUNE 17, 1942

Dear Diary,

A horrible thing happened today.

I was sitting alone on the porch after dinner when a man strolled by, walking a dog. He was tall and thin, and had very white skin. He let his dog sniff the bushes near our walkway. Then he glanced casually at me and said, "Nice night, no?" He had a foreign accent.

I nodded and said, "Yes, sir."

"It's nice to be sitting outside in the fresh air, to be free," he said. "Is it not?"

"Yes, sir."

He stared at me a moment, then slowly smiled. "A person wouldn't want to be in prison on a night like this, would they?" he said.

"I beg your pardon?" I said.

"Nobody would like to be arrested for treason when they could sit in the open air like this," he said. "Would they?"

The deepest chill went through me, like someone had dunked me in an ice-cold pond. I could only nod and whisper, "No, sir."

He smiled again. Then he pulled his dog along, and they kept walking, as if nothing were wrong, as if he hadn't just warned me that I might be sent to prison.

At that moment, Theo, Clara, and Miss Burke wandered out to the porch and began chatting about the weather. I couldn't join in because I felt like I was about to have a heart attack. I excused myself and headed up to my room. My knees felt like jelly as I climbed the stairs.

I got into bed, and though the room was hot, I pulled

up the covers and just lay there, trying not to melt with fear. Treason! Who was that guy? Was he connected to the Coast Guard?

Somehow Clara picked up on my feelings. She tapped on my door and asked if she could visit.

"Please," I begged, my teeth chattering.

She asked how I was feeling. I was dying to tell her everything, but I didn't dare.

I just told her I get scared sometimes. I told her I was scared for my dad and I was scared of people, too. I was scared of some strangers, I said.

She said she knew just how I felt. And I know she really did. More than anyone else in the world, Clara would understand the terror of strangers.

As I lay there, agonizing, she began singing a song in German. Her voice was as clear as a bell. It's a miracle she can sing at all when her life has been so horrible. My nightmare is nothing compared with Clara's. Yet, *she* comforts *me*.

Dear Diary,

I'm positively lucky to be alive.

I was riding my bike home from the Free Library today, and I was near the shore when a black car roared down the road. It swerved near me, making me lose control of my bike and crash into the curb. Then the darn driver of the car kept going, not even bothering to find out if I was okay!

I could hardly stand, my right leg was so painfully scraped up. My bicycle wheel was bent, so I was forced to leave my bike by the road and hobble toward home. Miraculously, Theo came by in his truck. I told him I'd carelessly run into the curb, and we went back for my bike. I didn't tell him about the car nearly hitting me, because I didn't want Mom to find out. It was just a little accident, but she'd have a fit.

Clara dressed my wounds, and Theo straightened out my bike wheel. Later, eating dinner with everyone, I felt especially lonesome. I was dying to come clean about what happened on the beach Friday night, and tell everyone about the man with the dog, and the black car on the road. I feel like my whole life is becoming a secret.

The fact is, I'm terrified. And I don't know what it's from, exactly. I mean, I won't get executed or anything. What I did wasn't *that* bad. Still, I'm terrified.

JUNE 20, 1942

Dear Diary,

I woke up with one clear thought in my head: I want to share my secrets with Johnny.

EVENING

Dear Diary,

All day I was as jumpy as a rabbit. I kept thinking, I've got to talk to Johnny before I explode.

But now I'm sweating over how to do it. I can't just walk up to his door and ask to talk to him. The Coast Guard might be following me. I might get his whole family in trouble if I'm seen visiting them.

This is nuts. I can go to Johnny's, doggone it. It's not against the law to walk up to a person's house and knock on their door. Golly, the United States is not a police state! It's not Hitler's Germany, for Pete's sake! I'm free to knock on a friend's door! My dad got wounded fighting for this freedom! Doggone it! Now I'm mad.

JUNE 21, 1942

Dear Diary,

Johnny wasn't home. He has a summer job as a pin boy at Palma's Bowling Lanes. His grandmother, though, seemed really happy to see me, and Bill hopped around, insisting I come look at the new flags on their map.

I took a quick peek, then asked Johnny's grandmother to give him a message when he came home. I gave her a piece of paper folded over. Inside it simply said: "Check the stump."

That was my first note. I put my second in the stump after I looked over my shoulder about a million times and didn't see any cars or people. The second note said: Eqog ugg Vjgq chvgt fkppgt. (Come see Theo after dinner.)

If the Coast Guard finds this note, they won't

understand its meaning. I'll stay on the lookout and waylay Johnny before he asks for Theo.

Right now I'm in my usual seat, peering out the window, watching for Johnny or for the man with the dog.

Theo and Clara are sitting in the porch swing. He's telling her that she should give singing lessons. She can use the piano in the parlor.

Right now Theo and Clara seem so innocent. They have no idea that I'm in the middle of a nightmare concerning top secret military activity.

My goodness! Johnny's riding up on his bike!

LATER

Dear Diary,

Johnny just left. On the way up to my room, I told him I was sorry for the way I'd been acting. I said there was no excuse for my mean behavior. He said yes, there was; I'd been upset about my dad. I could have hugged him for being so kind.

As soon as we got to my room, I didn't waste any more time. "Listen, I'm in serious danger," I said. "The Coast Guard's threatening me."

Johnny glanced around my room, as if expecting to see a nurse from an insane asylum.

I told him to sit down, so I could start from the beginning. Using my diary as a reference, I recalled every detail about the night I'd run into the secret Coast Guard operation. I told him all the strange things that have happened since.

When I finished, Johnny whistled, then said this sounded super serious.

I agreed. He wondered if the foreign speech I had heard could have been German. I said it was possible; then we both wondered if maybe the Coast Guard had caught a German saboteur. Johnny suggested that tomorrow we go back to the beach in broad daylight, when it's not off-limits. Then I could show him where I had stumbled onto the military operation.

I took a deep breath, worried I might be caught returning to the scene. But then that feeling of anger came over me. This is a *free* country, after all. "Why not?" I said.

"Good going, Colonel," he said, and he smiled that swell smile of his. I laughed, and for a quick moment, I did feel like my old self again.

It's time to hit the hay now. BIG day tomorrow.

JUNE 22, 1942

Dear Diary,

A scary discovery today!

Johnny came by on his bike while Mom and I were eating lunch. I told her we were going for a ride, and she looked really happy. I know she's been worried about my cutting myself off since we heard about Dad.

When I said good-bye to her, I felt guilty that Mom thought Johnny and I were heading out on a harmless bike ride when actually we were on a dangerous mission. But I have no choice. I have to keep facing the darkness. If I stand tall and face the thing I fear, I have a chance to conquer it. If I just keep dodging and hiding, it will conquer me.

We parked our bikes near the steps, then headed down the beach. We passed some kids playing in the sand, and grown-ups strolling in their swimsuits, but no men with bald heads or fedoras, and no Coast Guard.

Near the abandoned pier I showed Johnny the spot. He walked in circles, staring at the bright, silver-flecked sand as if he were Sherlock Holmes searching for footprints or a clue of some kind. I thought he was being silly, until he picked up something and called to me. When I ran over, he showed me a pack of cigarettes.

It was a pack of *German* cigarettes.

We both started talking excitedly. We figured maybe the Coast Guard *did* catch a German on the beach ten days ago. Jeepers, maybe the guy was a saboteur. Maybe he came off a U-boat.

The two of us stood in the white, glaring light of the sun, going over all these maybes.

Finally Johnny stuck the cigarette pack in his pocket. He had to hurry to his job at Palma's Bowling Lanes. But first he rode his bike with me all the way to the boardinghouse to make sure I got there safely.

Before we parted, we made a plan to meet tomorrow. I told him to be real careful on his way to Palma's. I even offered to go with him to make sure he was okay. He said then he'd have to ride back with me to make sure *I* was okay, and we'd end up going back and forth forever.

All through dinner, I debated whether or not I should at least tell Theo about our discovery of the German cigarettes. But I decided to keep my mouth shut. I'm still afraid that if I tell anyone in the house, I'll be putting myself in danger of treason. Plus, I positively don't want Mom to find out that I got into trouble with the Coast Guard. She's trying so hard not to fall apart because of Dad. One more terrible thing could give her a breakdown.

JUNE 23, 1942

Dear Diary,

I can't believe what I'm about to write. But this is what we discovered today, exactly what we discovered. (First, if anything happens to me — Mom, I love you so much, and Dad, I love you so much. And Clara, and everybody in this house — I love you all. Thank you for acting like my family. Oh, and I love the Roosevelts and our country so much, too.)

Okay, here's what happened:

Johnny came over after lunch, and we headed back to the scene of the military operation.

Again, no odd strangers or Coast Guard seemed to be on the scene. We ran barefoot over the hot sand, acting like two normal kids goofing around. When we got close to the pier, I suggested we explore the dunes.

We stopped to put on our shoes because the sand

around the dunes was really hot. As I was pulling on a sandal, I noticed a bunch of seaweed piled up nearby. I wondered aloud how it had gotten so high up on the beach.

Johnny wondered the same thing. He got a stick and began brushing away the sunbaked weeds. Soon he uncovered a shallow ditch in the sand. A wooden case bound with a rope was in the ditch. We used Johnny's pocketknife to cut the cord around the case, and when we opened it, we found a large tin inside. Inside the tin were a bunch of glass tubes and a sack of white powder.

We weren't sure what the powder and tubes were for. But we started poking around in the sand near the case, and the next thing we knew, we had uncovered two coats, and a pair of overalls, a pair of overshoes, and *three caps with Nazi swastikas.*

Johnny saw someone walking down the beach, coming our way. We quickly covered the stuff back up with seaweed and hid behind the dune. After a while, we peeked out, and the coast was clear.

We decided we'd better get the heck out of there. So we took off like lightning bolts and ran all the way back to the steps, jumped on our bikes, and hurried for home.

When we got to the crossroads, I turned and saw a black car following us. I screamed at Johnny to get off the road. We both leaped the curb and rode our bikes bumpily over the grass toward the baseball field. The black car drove on by. I couldn't tell if it was the same one that had almost hit me a few days ago or not. I might have just imagined it was after us. But I can't be sure.

When we got back to my place, Johnny and I zipped up to my room and sat on the floor and tried to get our bearings. He spoke first — and said exactly what I was thinking.

The facts are: We no longer think I ran into the Coast Guard at all. We think I ran into a band of Nazi saboteurs who had come ashore from a German U-boat. They buried their stuff in the sand, then disappeared. The Nazis are probably somewhere in the area right now, somewhere right here on Long Island. The powder in the case could be an explosive. They might be planning to come back for it and blow something up. Johnny and I think we are probably the only two Americans on earth who know this.

Furthermore, we think it was Nazi sympathizers who've been spying on me, who nearly hit me with the black car, and who warned me to be quiet!

Our plan now is for me to talk to Theo, not tell him what we know, but just ask him what *he* would do if he ever came across evidence that saboteurs were in the area. I'll tell him I need to know so I can tell K3F club members what to do in case such an unlikely event ever happens.

Theo's been fishing all day. I'm waiting for him in my room now, biting my nails off. I'm scared, but I've got to help our country for Dad's sake. Do it for Dad, do it for Dad, I keep telling myself. He sacrificed himself for America. Now it's my turn.

I just realized something. I'm actually in the middle of a "rendezvous with destiny," President Roosevelt's famous words. Mrs. Roosevelt's words taped on my wall fit my situation, too.

"You are going to have a great opportunity. There will be high moments in which your strength and ability will be tested. I have faith in you."

This *is* a great opportunity and a high moment, even though it doesn't feel that keen. It feels a little sickening. Actually, I feel nauseated. Victory does not come without a price.

LATER

Dear Diary,

Theo was great. I presented my "theoretical" situation to him and asked for advice.

He said there's only one thing he would do.

"What?" I breathed.

"Call the FBI," he said.

Golly, I couldn't imagine a better answer. I asked how a person called the FBI. He said it was listed in the phone book under Federal Bureau of Investigation.

"In our little phone book?" I asked.

He told me to wait, and he got his *Civil Defense Handbook* and found the FBI's number for me. He told me to give this to the kids in the club in case they ever needed it. That's what is so swell about Theo. He never acts like kids are too young for serious stuff like calling the FBI.

JUNE 24, 1942

Dear Diary,

Today I rode my bike to the hollow stump to leave a message for Johnny. I could swear someone was lurking down the road, but I left the note anyway. It said: Jcxg cpuygt!!

(Have answer!!)

Now I'm waiting for him to come over. My head's swimming with the facts. We've got to tell the FBI. But that seems impossible. Can two kids really get through to the FBI?

JUNE 25, 1942

Dear Diary,

Well, we did the impossible. We made our call from a pay phone near the bowling lanes. We had a bunch of coins, and we used up half of them before we even got an agent on the line.

I did all the talking. I tried to sound as adult as I could, lowering my voice and speaking calmly. I gave the basic facts, just the cold, hard facts of what I saw and what we found: the encounter on the beach, the cigarette pack, and the wooden case and clothes in the sand.

I didn't mention my life had been threatened. I was afraid the agent might think I was some crackpot who imagined danger all around her and was making up some story to explain it.

Finally I refused to give my name. I said, "I'm sorry, but I wish to remain anonymous."

The agent sounded only half-interested, though he asked for very detailed information about the location of everything. He didn't show one trace of excitement. In fact, he seemed bored! When I hung up, I was unsure of my success. But Johnny said that FBI agents are trained to sound bored.

Maybe so, but I feel a little let down. I mean, this was really big news as far as I was concerned. But I guess it was better for the guy to act calm; it was more professional.

Professional or not, I'm afraid the FBI agent's lack of excitement has thrown cold water on my own excitement. I'm wondering now if maybe I exaggerated the whole thing. Maybe the guy in the black car was just a reckless driver. Maybe the guy with the dog heard about me from some Coast Guard guy and was just making a joke. Maybe the stuff buried in the sand was . . . well, actually, it's hard to explain away that stuff on the beach, especially the three hats with swastikas.

What next?

I asked Johnny that before he headed off to Palma's. "We wait and see," he said.

I'm not a person who likes to wait and see. I prefer action, but I have no idea now what action to take.

Also, I'm afraid that while I wait I'll go back to worrying about Dad all the time. I'll start to lose my mind again.

JUNE 26, 1942

Dear Diary,

An odd thing has happened. Since Johnny and I called the FBI, I've stopped being afraid. I don't feel I'm being watched anymore. Either the saboteurs and their Nazi sympathizers have all left town — *or*, they never even existed. Telling my story to the FBI has somehow lifted a big burden off me.

Maybe I'm being foolish, but I feel safe now.

JUNE 27, 1942

Dear Diary,

It came today. It came when I wasn't looking. (Isn't that always the way? Like if you watch a pot of water that's about to boil, it *never* boils. Why is that?) Anyway, I was up in my room, reading a movie magazine, when it came. Mom was home for a change. I heard her loudly calling my name.

I hurried out to the landing, not guessing at all what had happened.

"Maddie! Maddie!" she kept shouting, and when I looked over the banister, I saw her waving a piece of paper. "A letter — a letter about Dad —" she screamed. Then she burst into sobs, happy sobs. You can always tell a happy sob from a sad one.

"He's okay —" she said, gasping. "Dad's okay —!"

I burst into happy sobs, too, and by the time I got my shaky, sobbing self down the stairs, the whole household was gathered around us, and *everyone* was crying. Even Theo had a tear on his cheek. Mrs. Hawkins and Miss Burke and Mrs. Rosenthal were crying. And Clara was crying! Miracles! Clara, who'd forgotten how to cry. We were all crying and at the same time, laughing at ourselves for crying.

It was the single most wonderful moment of my life.

JUNE 28, 1942

Dear Diary,

Mom and I have read the letter so many times, we know it by heart. A nurse wrote it from the navy hospital at Pearl Harbor, Hawaii. She said she was writing at Dad's request. She said he was recuperating from his injuries. She said he wanted us to know that his wounds were healing, and he did not want us to worry.

The nurse gave us the address where we should write him. Some of the letter was censored — big black marks through whole sentences. But now we know what we most needed to know. Dad's alive. He's recuperating.

We don't know why he didn't write the letter himself. Mom says we're not going to worry about that. She says it doesn't matter what his wounds are. The only thing that matters is that he's alive and we're going to be completely grateful for that. If there's anything to worry about, Mom says, we'll worry about it later.

JUNE 29, 1942

Dear Diary,

This morning I rode to the bowling lanes to tell Johnny the good news. He was setting up pins when I shouted at him, "My dad is safe!"

He grinned and dropped the pins and came running. The bowlers all hollered at him, but he came to me, anyway, and gave me a giant hug before running back to do his job.

JULY 1, 1942

Dear Diary,

In three days I've written five letters to Dad. I've told him everything (except about the saboteurs, of course, and my call to the FBI. I don't want to give him a heart attack).

I described the weather in detail and all the swell things people have said and done since hearing the good news about him. (Mrs. Hawkins made a blueberry pie for us all, and Miss Burke had an announcement put in the local paper!) I told him how much I loved him about twenty times and how sad Mom and I had been and how grateful we are now. I told him that I pray all the time we will see him very, very soon. I told him that I was sorry I had not written to him enough, and now he'll get more letters than he ever wanted.

JULY 2, 1942

Dear Diary,

It's a riot. Everyone's writing to Dad. Theo and Clara sent him a get-well card. Mrs. Hawkins and Miss Burke wrote him cheerful notes. I saw Maxine and the Star Points and Bert Lyman at the movies, and they said they all wanted to write him! Oh, this is the best — Johnny and Bill are sending him a package from their whole family with books and socks in it! Plus some Italian pastries made by Johnny's grandmother! Isn't that swell?

It's not like people don't know other soldiers in the battlefield. (Maxine has two uncles on their way to Europe, Johnny's cousins are in training now, and Theo knows at least three fishermen who've gone into the navy). But Dad was the first one anyone knows to be injured. So even though he's never set foot in this town, he's like a special "hometown boy." I'd better write him and explain who everyone is so he won't be completely baffled by all his mail.

I'll tell him that Mom's eyes shine like stars these days. I know she's counting every minute until we see him again.

JULY 3, 1942

Dear Diary,

I'm writing Dad twice a day. Mom and I are waiting anxiously to hear again from his nurse. It's been a week since her letter. If she only knew how much another letter would mean to us, surely she would take the time to write more often. (I said those exact words in my last letter to Dad, hoping when the nurse reads them to him, she'll get the message.)

JULY 4, 1942

Dear Diary,

I'm getting ready to go with Johnny, Bill, Theo, Clara, Mom, Miss Burke, Mrs. Hawkins, and even

Mrs. Rosenthal to the fireworks at the ball field. Never has a Fourth of July meant more. Freedom. Family. Friends.

JULY 6, 1942

Dear Diary,

Johnny and I made an amazing discovery today. It's been a little over two weeks since we found the Nazi stuff buried in the sand, and for the first time we went back to the beach to take another look. Guess what. We couldn't find anything. *Not one thing!* We looked and looked everywhere. There was no indication of a shallow ditch, a case, any clothes, or the three Nazi caps. It was all gone, the sand swept clean.

I left there, half-feeling we'd dreamed the whole thing. But Johnny swore we hadn't. He thinks the Nazis might have cleaned up the area. Or maybe the FBI did.

It's strange, but for some odd reason, neither of us seems that interested in the subject anymore. Our fear and suspicions seem to have all blown away with the evidence. I'm only dreaming of the day Dad comes home, and Johnny seems to be thinking mostly about his swell job at Palma's and the bike scavenger hunt on Saturday for the USO Fund.

On our ride home, we had a contest to see who could ride the longest without using their hands.

We sat on the porch with Theo and Clara. Johnny and Theo talked about shark fishing, while Clara and I talked about the marionette show at Guild Hall. Miss Burke has roped the two of us into being usherettes there tomorrow night. What will we wear is our big question.

JULY 8, 1942

Dear Diary,

I'm still in shock. Johnny came by today. He asked if I had seen the paper. I said I hadn't. He said we should go somewhere private.

I led him to a bench in the backyard, and he pulled out today's local paper and pointed at the headlines:

NAZI SABOTEURS LAND DYNAMITE ON BEACH FROM U-BOAT

My eyes nearly popped out of my head. I pressed my hands against my heart and said, "Oh, my gosh!"

It seems that on the night of June 12, four Nazi agents came ashore from a submarine off our coast. The FBI and the Coast Guard found explosives, detonators, and other equipment in the sand. The men had plans for a two-year program of destruction of industrial plants, railroads, waterworks, and bridges stretching from New York to the Ohio Valley.

All four saboteurs had worked in the United States at one time or another. They all spoke English and had been trained at a school for saboteurs in Berlin. They're all expected to be executed once they are convicted in court.

Then Johnny came to the last sentence in the article. It simply said: "Officials revealed that a call from an anonymous tipster helped lead them to the scene of the Nazi landing."

When Johnny finished reading that sentence, I fainted. It's true. I've never fainted before in my life, but I just keeled over, my head landing on Johnny's shoulder.

He slapped my cheeks just like they do in the movies, and I came to. He told me to bend over and put my head near my ankles, and I did.

When I sat up again, I had a roaring headache. I felt like throwing up, too. It was all too much. I told Johnny I had to go lie down, and he helped me to the back porch and called for my mom.

Clara came instead and ushered me inside, and I told Johnny I'd see him tomorrow. Clara helped me upstairs, and I fell on my bed, feeling like I was in a fever. I went to sleep and slept for the rest of the day and night.

I guess I'm not much of a colonel if I can't handle the consequences of my actions.

Did Johnny Vecchio and I change the course of history?

JULY 9, 1942

Dear Diary,

I feel like my life has been changed forever. But life at Mrs. Hawkins's Mansion-by-the-Sea goes on as usual. Everyone in the house sat on the porch today and discussed the Nazi landing on the beach. Theo said he wasn't surprised. Mom, Miss Burke, and Clara thought it sounded more like a movie than real life. Mrs. Rosenthal just knitted and smiled. (I was relieved she didn't seem terribly upset, as Theo once predicted she would. I think she feels safer in America now.)

Everyone tried to remember what they were doing that night. Nobody asked me what I was doing. As the daylight faded, I just listened silently as they all talked about it. I felt like a ghost who'd come back to Earth and was listening to the innocent, naive voices of people she loved.

Johnny must be feeling the same strangeness. Without even saying it, we seem to have both agreed that it's no use to try to convince people of our role in the capture of the criminals.

Isn't that what you learn in church — Do good works for their own sake and not for the reward? That's a tall order. I'm not sure I could follow that order if fate had decreed a choice. The fact is: Johnny and I positively have no choice. Even if we wanted to be famous for changing the course of history, no one would believe our story. If we told our friends or families that *we* were the "anonymous tipster," they'd think we were lying for sure.

JULY 13, 1942

Dear Diary,

Johnny's working nearly every day at Palma's. The K3F club is taking a break since school's out. But in our free time, Johnny, Bill, and I plan to do some stuff for the war effort, like collect more scrap and newspapers. In fact, Johnny and Bill are coming by tomorrow afternoon, so we can all go together to the bike scavenger hunt for the USO Fund.

On the hunt, we'll ride our bikes and try to collect all the things listed on a piece of paper. We're supposed to find things the USO club needs, like ashtrays, hand soap, and drinking cups. The person who finds the most things wins.

JULY 14, 1942

Dear Diary,

Bill Vecchio won the scavenger hunt! Out of the forty-five kids who participated, he brought in the most complete list. (I think because he's so young and enthusiastic, a lot of townspeople gave him a helping hand.)

It's no surprise what he said when they gave him his little trophy: "Holy smokes!"

During the hunt, fifteen servicemen were brought to the USO Hall because the list called for "a man in uniform." They were all great sports. At the end of the day, the women's auxiliary sponsored a little party with a band and punch and cookies.

Theo, Clara, and Miss Burke came by. When the Four Hearts played a dance tune, Theo and Clara danced, and even with Theo's limp, they made a lovely couple, both dressed in white. Theo asked Miss Burke to dance the jitterbug. She laughed and said no, but I thought it was nice of Theo to ask.

Johnny was shy at first. But after about the third tune, he asked me to dance to "Taking a Chance on Love." He held me close as we clumsily stepped together around the room. We passed some grown-ups talking about the Nazi saboteurs and we didn't even poke or nudge each other. I think for some reason the truth scares us both to death.

JULY 17, 1942

Dear Diary,

Finally another letter from one of Dad's nurses! This one told us more about his condition. His hands were burned, so they are in bandages and that's why he can't write to us himself. His head injury is not completely healed, so he can't think as clearly as he'd like to. But he can understand all our letters, she wrote, and when she and others read them to him, he lights up like a candle.

Mom broke down when she read these touching words — "He lights up like a candle." And she sobbed over Dad's injuries. When I tried to comfort her, she kept sobbing. She said Dad must be suffering so much. "Burns are so painful!" she cried.

Even though I was crying, too, I told her we'd be with him soon. I told her we'd help heal his burns and his wounds. I said we'd touch him and talk to him and dance for him to help him get better. I kept talking and talking, saying anything to try to stop Mom's grief. I didn't worry a bit about prying.

One thing I know very deeply now: War is not about fun and games. It's about terrible sadness, pain, and fear.

JULY 21, 1942

Dear Diary,

My words to Mom have come true. A doctor from Dad's hospital wrote us today. He said we could be with Dad soon. He said they expect Dad to fully recover and resume his military duties someday. But it may take some time, and for that reason, they are sending him back to the states, to a hospital at the naval base in San Francisco.

At the hospital, they plan to have a bedside ceremony for Dad, to give him an Air Medal. If Mom and I move to San Francisco, we can attend the award ceremony and visit Dad every day.

I imagine he'll be a bit of a stranger to us at first. He'll be changed from his war experiences and from his wounds. But for that matter, Mom and I won't be the same people he knew before, either. We've both grieved our hearts out and fought our secret wars.

JULY 22, 1942

Dear Diary,

Mom quit her job at the defense factory today, so we can leave by Friday. Friday's just two days away.

We have to leave that soon, Mom says, so we can get to San Francisco and find a rooming house by the time Dad arrives. We'll get a train from New York City to Chicago, then another from Chicago to San Francisco. The trains are so full of servicemen these days, we might have long waits at the stations.

Mom explained these plans to everyone at dinner, and I saw tears in people's eyes. Mom herself wept a little and said, "Now, now, we'll write. We'll be back. And someday, you must all come to visit us — wherever we are."

But I know the truth. When you live a military life, you don't see people again. And you stop writing them after a short time. You just move along and make new friends. Then you move along again.

This time it feels especially sad, though. Maybe it's because of the war. Our "family unit" has become like a real family. Talking on the porch at night or gathered around the dinner table, we take a lot of comfort in each other. Why, right now I feel as close to Theo and Clara as if they were my big brother and sister. How can I say good-bye to them?

And Johnny . . . How the heck can I say good-bye to Johnny?

JULY 23, 1942

Dear Diary,

I rode my bike to Johnny's house this morning to tell him the news. I asked if I could speak to him alone. In case I cried, I didn't want his grandmother or Bill to see me.

We sat on his back steps and I told him Dad was getting an Air Medal.

"He deserves it," Johnny said softly.

Then I told him Mom and I would be leaving tomorrow to go live in San Francisco.

Johnny sucked in his breath and looked away from me. He didn't say anything for a long moment.

"So I guess this is good-bye," I said.

Still, without looking at me, he reached out and

grabbed my hand. He held it real tight. He squeezed it and didn't look at me. That's when a tear started down my cheek.

"I'll miss you, Mad," he whispered.

"Me, you," I whispered back.

Then he sighed and looked at me. He had a tear or two on his cheeks. He leaned over and kissed me.

But I had to blow my nose, so I couldn't linger long in that position. I sniffed and asked for a tissue.

Johnny jumped up and went inside. When he came back a minute later with the Kleenex box, his grandmother and brother were with him.

They both hugged me and said they'd miss me. His grandmother told me to write, and I told her I would.

As I started to leave, Johnny said he'd come by tonight after work to see me one last time.

LATER

Right now Mom's at the church saying good-bye to her friends. I just finished packing. It's not quite dark. I'm about to go downstairs and sit with everyone on the porch. Theo will report on the number of bluefish he caught today. Miss Burke will gossip about something, and we'll all talk about what my life in San Francisco will be like.

When it grows dark, Johnny will show up on his bike and join us. I have the feeling that he and I will hold hands. Right now the radio is playing "I'll Be Seeing You in All the Old, Familiar Places." Will Johnny think of me when he hears that song in the future?

The bond between me and Johnny is more special than most bonds. We're the only two people in the world who know the truth about how the saboteurs were caught. If one of us dies one day, the other will have to bear the secret alone. Except maybe I'll tell my children. Children always believe their parents, at least the small ones do.

Maybe Johnny will tell Bill. I suspect Bill will believe our secret, too. He has the heart of a hero, and believes the best about everybody. "Holy smokes," he'll say.

I've known another person this year who has the heart of a hero: Clara Rosenthal. Clara had her first singing student today, and I think it went very well. One thing haunts me: The day we got the great news about Dad, Clara cried for the first time in years. *Her* father will never come home to her, yet she cried with joy because *my* dad was coming home to me.

Theo said Clara had faced the darkness and won the war. I know now what he meant. Though the war seems far from over, Clara has already defeated the Nazis. With all their storm troopers and bombs and U-boats, they could not kill this one seemingly small thing: Clara Rosenthal's goodness.

It gives me hope for myself. It gives me hope for the whole world.

Epilogue

Maddie Beck took the long train ride to San Francisco with her mother and was happily reunited with her father. Captain Beck's wounds prevented him from flying again during the war, but he did recover well enough to remain in the navy. Over the next few years, Maddie attended school at a number of naval bases. She graduated from high school while stationed near Virginia Beach, Virginia.

Contrary to her prediction, Maddie and her mother *did* remain in close touch with the household of Mrs. Hawkins's Mansion-by-the-Sea. In fact, Theo and Clara got married and named their first child Maddie in honor of their friend.

Maddie went back to meet her namesake the summer after her senior year in high school. She and Johnny Vecchio began dating that summer. And to no one's surprise, they became engaged two years later.

After graduating from college (Maddie from Mary Washington College in Fredericksburg, Virginia, and Johnny from Georgetown University in Washington, D.C.), Johnny and Maddie were married in the summer of 1949. They settled in Washington, D.C., where Johnny worked for many years for *National Geographic* magazine, and Maddie worked as an organizer for the American Red Cross.

LIFE IN AMERICA
IN 1941–1942

Historical Note

World War II began two years before the United States joined the fight. From 1939 until 1941, while Americans watched helplessly, Adolf Hitler's German troops invaded country after country in Europe. One of the most horrendous aspects of Hitler's brutality was his campaign against Jews and other minorities. After the war, it was learned that over 8 million European Jews had been murdered by the Nazis. The annihilation of the Jews came to be called the Holocaust.

During the time of Hitler's aggression, the nation of Japan was also seeking to expand its empire. It had moved into Indochina and was planning to conquer other parts of the Pacific. When the Japanese attacked the U.S. military base at Pearl Harbor, Hawaii, on December 7, 1941, the United States was finally brought into World War II. The United States declared war against Japan and, quickly thereafter, against Germany.

Once the United States got involved in World War II, the nation threw itself wholeheartedly into the struggle. Inspired by President Franklin Delano Roosevelt and First Lady Eleanor Roosevelt, millions of Americans "fought the war" on the home front. Thousands of women went to work in defense factories and shipyards to help make weapons and ammunition, ships and planes. Children ran scrap metal drives, fat drives, and book drives. Civilians trained to be auxiliary firemen, policemen, nurses' aides, and air-raid wardens. They served as plane-spotters and had Victory Gardens. Women stopped wearing silk and nylon stockings so that silk and nylon could be used to make parachutes and medical supplies. Families sacrificed gasoline, sugar, meat, rubber, tinfoil, and many other things to help in the war effort.

While Americans sacrificed on the home front, great numbers of military men and women were sacrificing abroad. In the Pacific alone, more than one hundred thousand American sailors and marines were wounded and more than five hundred naval ships were sunk.

America was the only major power whose land was not physically shattered by the war. There were times, however, when the enemy was close to American soil.

Japanese submarines sometimes operated off the Pacific coast of the United States; and in the early months of the war, German submarines, known as U-boats, patrolled the Atlantic Coast of the United States. The U-boats sank a number of Allied ships during the winter and early spring of 1942.

Eventually, the U.S. Navy and Coast Guard developed ways to detect and sink the German submarines, and the U-boat threat declined. On June 12, 1942, however, two German U-boats delivered eight Nazi saboteurs onto American soil. One group of four landed in north Florida, and the other landed near the tip of Long Island, New York. The four Nazis who landed on Long Island buried boxes of explosives in the sand, planning to destroy American industrial companies and transportation facilities. Eventually the saboteurs were turned in by two of their own group, and all but the two informers were executed.

In 1945, World War II ended in victory for the United States and its Allies. In May of that year, Germany surrendered; in August, Japan surrendered. Altogether, more than 57 million people had been killed in the war.

The December 8, 1941, edition of The New York Times *announces the December 7 bombing of the United States military base in Pearl Harbor, Hawaii. This attack led the U.S. to declare war against Japan, and soon after, against Germany.*

During the attack on Pearl Harbor, the U.S.S. Shaw's *magazine was hit, detonating ammunition and explosives held there.*

The U.S.S. Lexington, *a navy aircraft carrier, was badly damaged during the Battle of the Coral Sea on May 7–8, 1942. This battle was an indication of a new kind of warfare, in which dive bombers and torpedo planes would cause most of the damage; enemy ships never came in sight of one another.*

President Franklin Roosevelt declared that there was "one front and one battle where everyone in the United States — every man, woman, and child — is in action. That front is right here at home." Here, President Roosevelt with Eleanor Roosevelt, whose public service endeavors led to changes improving the welfare of American soldiers, and increased assistance for women who went to work to support the war effort and their families.

In response to President Roosevelt's message, American civilians eagerly accepted their role in World War II. In spite of wartime hardships, the collective efforts of rationing, recycling, and carpooling made many people feel more united with their fellow Americans than at any other time in history. Here, a group of Manhattan children called the Tin Can Club of America salvages cans for the war effort.

Rubber was necessary for the production of airplanes and tanks, but Japan controlled the Southeast Asian plantations that were the world's largest source of natural rubber. In June of 1942, President Roosevelt called on American citizens to turn in "old tires, old raincoats, old garden hose, rubber shoes, bathing caps, gloves." Across the country, groups emerged with the sole purpose of collecting rubber. Top, organized by the North and South Lawndale Citizens Defense Youth Organization, this enthusiastic group of Chicago children went collecting from house to house with bicycles and wagons. Bottom, one hundred and six trucks carrying more than eighty tons of rubber are led by members of a Boy Scout troop in Stevens Point, Wisconsin.

This ad encouraged people to plant a Victory Garden to supplement their wartime rations. Each household was issued ration books that held coupons for weekly and monthly allotments of items like meat, butter, cooking fat, shoes, and gasoline.

Along with food, rubber, and tin, the war effort also needed money. War bonds, which could be purchased for $18.75 and turned in after ten years for $25, covered one-sixth of the nation's $304 billion war expenses.

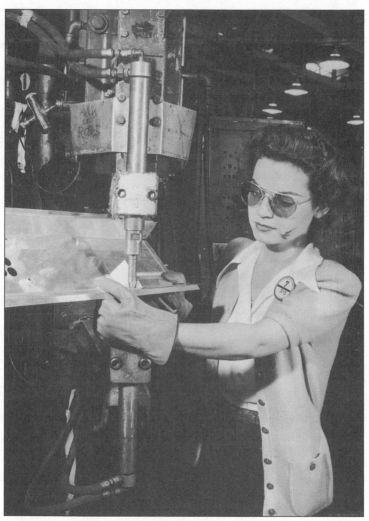

The United States government drew women to defense-industry jobs with ads reading, "If you've sewed on buttons, or made buttonholes on a machine, you can learn to do spot welding on airplane parts." Because defense jobs gave them a sense of responsibility for the war effort, women responded enthusiastically. Here, a woman works in the spot welding department for Lockheed, an aircraft manufacturer.

During World War II, millions of Americans joined the Red Cross effort as volunteers in the Nurse's Aide Corps, the Gray Lady Service, the Junior Red Cross, the Hospital and Recreation Corps, and in other services benefitting the armed services and the war effort.

Americans volunteered to serve as plane spotters and ground observers. This young girl works at the observation post of the Bangor, Maine Filter Center, where she reports on multi-motored aircraft, aircraft formations, aircraft that can be heard but not seen, and "unusual occurrences and unusual objects," such as "blimps, helicopters, balloons, accidents, strange objects."

Top, *the June 12, 1942, edition of the* Journal American *announces the landing of two German U-boats,* bottom, *on American soil; one in Florida and one on Long Island, New York. Four Nazis buried boxes of explosives on a Long Island beach, intending to return, and with them, destroy industrial companies and transportation facilities.*

176

REMEMBER PEARL HARBOR

☆ ☆ ☆

History, in every century,
records an act that lives
forevermore.
We'll recall, as into line we fall,
the thing that happened on
Hawaii's shore.

Let's remember Pearl Harbor
as we go to meet the foe.
Let's remember Pearl Harbor
as we did the Alamo.

We will always remember
how they died for liberty.
Let's remember Pearl Harbor
and go on to victory.

"Remember Pearl Harbor" was based on a popular World War II saying and became an instant hit with the public. It was played by every radio station and was sung at social, family, and religious gatherings across the country.

WAR CAKE

★ ★ ★

1 c. brown sugar	1½ c. flour
1 c. water	½ t. salt
1 c. raisins	½ t. baking powder
2 T. margarine	½ t. baking soda
1 t. cinnamon	½ c. chopped walnuts
½ t. ground cloves	

Preheat the oven to 350° F. Grease and flour an 8" x 4" baking pan. Place the brown sugar, water, raisins, margarine, cinnamon, and cloves in a heavy-bottomed saucepan and bring to a boil. Turn down heat and cook gently for 5 minutes. Remove from heat and let cool until the mixture is lukewarm. Sift together the flour, salt, baking powder, and baking soda. Add flour mixture to the cooled sugar mixture, beating until the batter is smooth. Stir in the walnuts. Spread evenly in the baking pan and bake for 25 to 30 minutes or until a toothpick inserted in the center of the cake comes out clean. Let cool in the pan 10 minutes, then turn onto a rack to cool completely.

Because sugarcane could be converted into gunpowder, sugar was among the staples that were rationed. Creative cooks baked War Cake, which required less sugar than a standard cake recipe, and no eggs or milk.

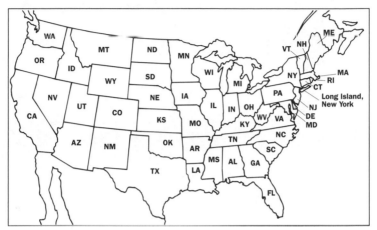

This modern map of the United States shows the location of Long Island, New York.

ABOUT THE AUTHOR

MARY POPE OSBORNE's father, like Madeline Beck's, was a career military officer. "Growing up in the fifties and sixties, my brothers and I often heard stories from our dad about his WWII experiences in New Guinea and stories from our mom about waiting for him on the home front," she says.

"I first heard about Nazi U-boats patrolling in American waters while we were living on an army base on the coast of Virginia. As my brothers and I played on the abandoned coastal artillery emplacements once used to defend the shore, we imagined what it would have been like to confront the enemy on the beach. Many years later, I read that Nazi saboteurs had actually come ashore on Long Island in 1942. That story captured my imagination and I seized upon it as the centerpiece of Maddie's story."

Mary Pope Osborne has written many books, in

almost every genre, for children and young adults. Her impressive backlist includes the Magic Tree House series, and, most recently, her novel *Adaline Falling Star* (Scholastic Press, 2000). For the Dear America Series, she is the author of *Standing in the Light: The Captive Diary of Catharine Carey Logan*, and for the My America series, *My Brother's Keeper: Virginia's Diary*. She lives in New York City with her husband, Will.

To the memory of my father,
Colonel William P. Pope,
who served in the Pacific during WWII

ACKNOWLEDGMENTS

I am deeply grateful to Robert Schnare, Jr., director of the Naval War College Library, for his tremendous research assistance; and to Tracy Mack, my editor, for her invaluable editing and inspiration.

Grateful acknowledgment is made for permission to reprint the following:

Cover portrait: Super Stock.
Cover background: FPG International.

Page 166: *The New York Times*, Culver Pictures.
Page 167: U.S.S. *Shaw*, Ewing Galloway.
Page 168 (top): U.S.S. *Lexington*, AP/Wide World Photos.
Page 168 (bottom): Franklin and Eleanor Roosevelt, Corbis/UPI.
Page 169: The Tin Can Club of America, AP/Wide World Photos.
Page 170 (top): Chicago children, AP/Wide World Photos.
Page 170 (bottom): Trucks carrying rubber, AP/Wide World Photos.
Page 171: Victory Garden, Stock Montage.
Page 172: War bonds, Stock Montage.
Page 173: Woman welder, Ewing Galloway.
Page 174: American Red Cross Ambulance, Ewing Galloway.
Page 175: Ground observers, U.S. Civil Defense.

OTHER BOOKS IN THE DEAR AMERICA SERIES

A Journey to the New World
The Diary of Remember Patience Whipple
by Kathryn Lasky

The Winter of Red Snow
The Revolutionary War Diary of Abigail Jane Stewart
by Kristiana Gregory

When Will This Cruel War Be Over?
The Civil War Diary of Emma Simpson
by Barry Denenberg

A Picture of Freedom
The Diary of Clotee, a Slave Girl
by Patricia McKissack

Across the Wide and Lonesome Prairie
The Oregon Trail Diary of Hattie Campbell
by Kristiana Gregory

So Far from Home
The Diary of Mary Driscoll, an Irish Mill Girl
by Barry Denenberg

I Thought My Soul Would Rise and Fly
The Diary of Patsy, a Freed Girl
by Joyce Hansen

West to a Land of Plenty
The Diary of Teresa Angelino Viscardi
by Jim Murphy

Dreams in the Golden Country
The Diary of Zipporah Feldman
by Kathryn Lasky

A Line in the Sand
The Alamo Diary of Lucinda Lawrence
by Sherry Garland

Standing in the Light
The Captive Diary of Catharine Carey Logan
by Mary Pope Osborne

Voyage on the Great Titanic
The Diary of Margaret Ann Brady
by Ellen Emerson White

My Heart Is on the Ground
The Diary of Nannie Little Rose, a Sioux Girl
by Ann Rinaldi

The Great Railroad Race
The Diary of Libby West
by Kristiana Gregory

The Girl Who Chased Away Sorrow
The Diary of Sarah Nita, a Navajo Girl
by Ann Turner

A Light in the Storm
The Civil War Diary of Amelia Martin
by Karen Hesse

A Coal Miner's Bride
The Diary of Anetka Kaminska
by Susan Campbell Bartoletti

Color Me Dark
The Diary of Nellie Lee Love
by Patricia McKissack

One Eye Laughing, the Other Weeping
The Diary of Julie Weiss
by Barry Denenberg

While the events described and some of the characters
in this book may be based on actual historical events
and real people, Madeline Beck is a fictional character,
created by the author, and her diary and its epilogue
are works of fiction.

Library of Congress Cataloging-in-Publication Data
Osborne, Mary Pope.
My secret war: the World War II diary of Madeline Beck /
Mary Pope Osborne.
p. cm. — (Dear America)
Summary: Thirteen-year-old Madeline's diaries for 1941 and 1942
reveal her experiences living on Long Island during World War II
while her father is away in the navy.
ISBN 0-590-68715-8
1. World War, 1939–1945 — New York (State) — Juvenile fiction.
[1. World War, 1939–1945 — United States — Fiction.   2. New York (State) —
Fiction.   3. Diaries — Fiction.]   I. Title.   II. Series.
PZ7.O81167 My 2000
[Fic] — dc21   00-021918
CIP   AC
10 9 8 7 6 5 4 3 2 1   03 04 05 06 07

The display type was set in Bernhard Gothic.
The text type was set in Janson Text.
Book design by Elizabeth B. Parisi

Printed in the U.S.A.   23
First printing, September 2000

Reinforced Library Edition
ISBN 0-439-55512-4
November 2003